When Britt O'Connor's targeted by a group of mercenaries for reasons unknown, he realizes it's time to cash in a big favor. Britt heads to World of Aquatica. He knows that's where his ex-SEAL buddy, Price, has secretly holed up after Britt helped him flee the military police. Britt also knows that Price isn't human, and he could use a little of the man's paranormal abilities right about then.

Getting there is easy. Getting inside and locating Price is a bit more difficult. Still, Britt manages it, only to discover that Price isn't the only paranormal thing at the park. Vampires and shifters are real. In fact, not only does Price vouch for him, but Britt meets Gerard, a shifter who claims he's the other half of his soul.

When Gerard scents Britt as he's on his way to meet with Alpha Kaiser, he immediately recognizes him as his mate and follows him. Discovering that Britt already knows about the paranormal, he declares that Britt is his mate, but Britt will need some convincing.

While Britt can accept being attracted to the shifter, after all the depravity Britt has seen, how can he trust in something as fickle as love?

Scuba Diving with a Sea Dragon
Copyright © 2022 Charlie Richards
ISBN:
Cover art by Angela Waters

Published by eXtasy Books Inc

Look for us online at:
www.eXtasybooks.com

Scuba Diving with a Sea Dragon
Beneath Aquatica's Waves:
Book Fourteen

By

Charlie Richards

DEDICATION

We only get so much time in this world. Don't squander it.
~Unknown

CHAPTER ONE

"What the hell?"

Growling under his breath, Britt O'Connor stared at his readout. He started typing rapidly, his fingers flying over the keys. Britt clenched his jaw as he worked to counter the hacker trying to break into his system . . . and failing.

Britt knew he was an excellent hacker. Hell, after he'd left the military, he'd chosen to utilize his skills to make his livelihood. Technically, Britt was listed as an analyst for a security firm, but he took the occasional anonymous side job. Still, Britt knew it was the hubris of man to think he could be the best, and he would never fall into that trap.

There's always someone better out there.

Whoever Britt was facing — as much as it galled him to admit — was one of those people. They were better. Before long, they would break into his heavily encrypted system.

That meant Britt had to make certain there was nothing left to find. At the same time, if he could manage it, he would implant a reverse worm. The code would allow him to backtrack to the user, allowing him to see where they were located, and perhaps, if he was lucky, he would see a signature revealing who the hacker might be.

Worth a shot.

Continuing to type with his right hand, Britt reached over and grabbed a flash drive with his left. He paused an instant to find the slot and insert it. Then, while Britt did his best to delay the hacker from entering his system, he began directing sensitive files to the drive.

Britt felt sweat bead at his temples, and his fingers began to cramp. At fifty-four years old, he was lucky he hadn't acquired arthritis in his wrists and digits. Still, he didn't usually have to work quite so quickly.

Finally, Britt had pulled as much sensitive information off his desktop as possible. He knew he was only a couple of moments away from being breached. After encrypting everything on the drive, he removed it from the machine. Britt activated a failsafe he'd designed but had hoped never to have to use.

In seconds, Britt's entire hard drive was wiped clean. He grabbed his laptop and shoved it into his bag. Hurrying around the room, Britt snagged a few other necessary electronics. With a backpack on his back and his laptop bag's strap over his shoulder, he made his way to his basement.

Britt knelt before a set of dusty-looking wooden shelves. Reaching under the bottom, he pried up a board and set it aside. He pulled out a large *go bag* with guns, ammunition, a couple changes of clothes, as well as money, and a couple of different IDs and passports. Britt replaced the board and used an old hand-brush hanging on the wall—left there for that reason—to kick up some dust, hiding the evidence.

With his bags in hand, Britt crossed to another wall. He picked up a can of paint off the floor, revealing a stone panel. When Britt stepped on it, a section of wall that looked like stone rotated ninety degrees, revealing a dark corridor.

Britt replaced the can of paint exactly, pulled a flashlight from his belt, and headed into the dark expanse.

If my systems have been breached, I need to know if my anonymity has been compromised, too.

In Britt's mind, the best way to do that was to hide in the area and watch.

Not twelve hours later, Britt sat in a tiny tree stand and watched a dozen armed men creep toward his mountain home. He couldn't see their faces since they were covered with hoods. However, the weapons they were carrying gave them away.

They were mercenaries from South America.

The softly spoken Spanish dialect spouted by their team leader was an obvious tell, too.

Britt heard him issuing orders to Bravo Team to secure the perimeter. Echo Team was supposed to guard the backdoor in case Britt fled. His own Alpha Team was getting ready to breach the front door.

The fact that the leader had referred to Britt as *Escritor Fantasma* — or Ghostwriter — also gave him a lead as to who might be coming after him. That was one of several handles he used when dealing with off-the-books works. Deals that were of questionable legality.

Still, if the information I provide takes down a corrupt politician, businessman, or a group of cops on the take, I don't mind helping out.

So, who did I piss off that has the connections to find me?

Britt knew that was the multi-million-dollar question. His research had made no shortage of enemies. It also meant he had no idea who he could trust to help him figure it out.

Turning away from where the commandos were storming his home, Britt figured the obvious would be out. After all, if these guys knew where he lived, then they probably knew where he worked. They would also know who he worked with.

And I don't want to drag any of them down due to some work I did on the side.

That left Britt on his own.

Creeping from one branch to the next, Britt stayed aware of his footwork. He'd left most of his supplies in his hidden getaway vehicle hours before. Then he'd crept to his hidden tree stand to watch and wait.

As much as the information Britt had gleaned sucked, it

had paid off. He had a direction to start searching in. Britt would find a place to hole up and figure it out.

When Britt was over a mile away from the mountain retreat he'd called home for over a decade, he finally reached his hidden vehicle. He'd stashed it on an old logging road that wasn't on a map and wasn't easily accessible unless one knew the area. Britt had hiked everywhere around within a ten-mile radius.

After Britt slipped behind the wheel of the old, beat-up-looking *Ford Bronco*, he rested his rifle against the front seat. Then he fired up the vehicle. While the exterior was beat to shit, making it easy to blend in with the rural area, the engine in the machine was in tip-top shape.

Britt headed out.

Forty minutes of back roads took Britt over twenty-five miles away from those after him. He made it to the highway and paused, looking left and right, weighing his options. Did he head to a big city to hide in anonymity? Or should he stay under the radar by living off the grid? Britt had supplies for either option in the back of his vehicle.

Hmmm . . . how about anonymity and *off the grid?*

Time to call in a favor.

Recalling the time Britt had helped a friend, he headed west.

Three days of driving along back roads and sleeping in the car found Britt where he needed to be. He followed the signs for *World of Aquatica* and turned off the highway. The California coast boasted slightly drizzly weather, but the parking lot for the marine park was still packed.

Britt continued along the road, sweeping his gaze over the area. He spotted a huge wooden arch boasting sea creatures of all manner upon it. Continuing past the park, Britt knew the massive place also offered living amenities to those who worked at the park and their families.

And that's where I'll find the thought deceased Price Litner.

In truth, Britt didn't know if Price had created a new identity. He knew the man had been reported as deceased up in Alaska, having been followed there by a vindictive military police officer. There, according to eyewitnesses, Price had been swept out to sea by a giant octopus.

Britt knew that was bogus, though. He knew Price had . . . abilities — paranormal abilities. Britt wasn't one hundred percent certain what Price was, but if he had to guess, he would say the man was a vampire. The guy hadn't aged at all in the thirty years he'd known him. In fact, he'd even found a picture or two of Price from years before Britt had met him, and he still damn near looked the same.

Vampires didn't age, right?

Then there was the blood thing. The man had been flagged by the military police after a blood test came out wonky. A human didn't go from O-negative blood to O-positive blood. It just didn't happen.

Then Price had revealed that he always faked his blood draws.

If Price was a vampire, that would make sense. He couldn't very well have blood anomalies showing up on tests.

Britt knew that Price had gone to his old army buddy — Graham Canton — for help. That meant there was a good chance he'd returned there after faking his death.

If not, I bet Graham can tell me where Price ended up.

With that hope in mind, Britt located a side road with an electronic gate. He parked before it and eyed the keypad. From his research about the place, he'd discovered a few codes that could open it. Picking one, Britt punched it in and entered the grounds.

Britt had every intention of finding a discreet place to park his *Bronco* before hiking back toward the marine park. He knew he would run into the structures of employee living on the way.

"There ya go, mates," Gerard called, grinning widely as he swept his gaze over the enthralled crowd. "Give a warm round of applause for Tony the tiger shark," he encouraged, indicating the large shark circling the massive tank.

Immediately, the sold-out crowd—even on a cold, drizzly afternoon—erupted into hoots, hollers, and applause. Even after being in operation for over a decade, the tiger shark show was still *World of Aquatica*'s biggest attraction. Nowhere else in the world put on a show quite like theirs—having a tiger shark jump through hoops and into the air for meat.

Of course, no one knows that we're shifters, and the shark we call Tony is actually a paranormal named Tort.

Tort shared the tiger shark show responsibilities with two other tiger shark shifters—River and Caden. Caden had handled the morning show, and River was scheduled the following morning with Caden in the afternoon. They rotated the shows, giving them breaks.

Grinning widely, Gerard rested his hands on his hips. "Just as a reminder, Tony will be heading into the underground sunken ship exhibit." He swept his gaze over the group, keeping an eye out for trouble as people started moving toward the exits. "He'll be there with plenty of other wonderful specimens for your viewing pleasure."

"Isn't it dangerous to have the shark in with so many other animals?" a slender brunette woman asked, stopping next to him. Her smile appeared shy even as she peered at him coyly through her lashes. "I mean"—she lifted a hand and touched her lower neck, drawing attention to her low-cut shirt—"won't the shark eat the other animals?"

Considering that Gerard had seen just about every pick-up line possible, he decided this woman's approach was rather tame. Of course, the fact that there were plenty of children running around was probably one of the reasons. He was flattered, a little, even though he didn't have any interest in her.

Gerard preferred redheads.

"In each of our aquariums, we provide a natural habitat for every animal," Gerard explained to the brunette, keeping his smile relaxed and easy without a hint of encouragement. "That means there are plenty of places for the animals to hide, just like in the wild." Pointing toward where a canal had opened, which Gerard knew led to the underwater aquarium, he added, "Plus, he just had a number of slabs of tasty meat, so he won't be lookin' for anythin' anytime soon."

"Oh, of course," the woman responded with a soft giggle. "I bet you know—"

Whatever she thought he knew, Gerard would never know. He spotted a group of kids shoving their way down the stadium's stairs. Growling under his breath, he felt a flash of déjà vu.

Damn teenagers.

"Excuse me," Gerard rumbled, lifting a hand by way of apology. In the next instant, he hurried toward the stairs on the left. "The sign says *walk* for a reason," Gerard called forcefully, scowling up at the descending teenagers. When they yanked their attention away from each other to focus on him, Gerard immediately spotted the curl of the bigger boy's lip. He decided to nip that in the bud and pinned the ringleader with a cold look. "What if, in your hurry, your pretty girlfriend slipped, fell, and cracked her head on these stone steps?" Dipping his chin, he indicated the stadium stairs. "Ya wouldn't want anythin' to happen to her, would ya?"

In his peripheral vision, Gerard noticed the widening of the dark-haired teenage girl's eyes, who held the guy's hand. She nibbled her bottom lip and quickly looked away. Her cheeks took on a pinkish hue.

"Whatever," the guy muttered. "I wouldn't've let her fall."

"We're sorry, sir," the girl murmured, focusing on him

again. "We'll walk." After a few seconds of nibbling her bottom lip some more, she nudged her shoulder into the guy's arm. "Let's go, Mike."

Gerard took a step backward and to the side, getting out of their way. "Have fun, guys," he rumbled, sweeping his attention over the other pair — another male-female teenage couple. "And stay safe."

They wasted no time in hurrying past him.

Gerard ignored the antagonist's angry glare over his shoulder at him.

Gods. Kids these days. I hope my mate doesn't end up wanting any.

Spotting Kyger near the entrance, Gerard began making his way toward his buddy, a barracuda shifter. He paused near a railing and waited. That allowed him to keep an eye on Kyger as well as the rest of the crowd.

"Hey, Kyger," Gerard greeted without truly meeting the dark-haired shifter's gaze. "How ya doin', man?"

Kyger stopped next to him and leaned against the railing. "I'm good. Dolbert and Rigelle are on clean-up duty." He watched the others stream past. "You okay? You seem a little . . . tense."

Gerard heaved a sharp breath. "Yeah," he grumbled even as he shook his head. "Just had to stop some dipshit teenagers from sendin' another person down the stairs."

A couple of years prior, Tort had met his human mate, Kane, when some dick teenagers had pushed Kane into the aquarium. Sure, it had been a mistake, but it had instigated a number of changes. First, a safety screen had been put up from the ground to three feet up, even though it could obstruct the views of the first few rows. New policies and procedures were put in place, giving Gerard authority to detain or toss out guests who were running or misbehaving without fear of reprisal from his bosses.

While Gerard appreciated it, he didn't particularly enjoy

confronting humans. He would rather be seen as the friendly announcer and approached with questions. Still, he knew safety at a marine park was paramount.

"Damn, I'm sorry, Gerard." Kyger patted him on the back. "You know that no one blames you for what happened to Kane back in the day."

Scoffing, Gerard pinned his buddy with a wry smile. "I know. And I don't, either."

"Does that mean you're still up for a hike?"

Gerard nodded. "Yeah. Let's head up to the condos so I can change." He peered down at his *World of Aquatica* work shirt and khaki shorts before smirking at Kyger. "Not hikin' in this."

Kyger laughed. "I don't blame you."

The pair exited the stadium, passing Dolbert and Rigelle on the way.

Five minutes later, Gerard rounded a curve in the sidewalk and spotted the large apartment and condominium complex. He picked up his pace, eager for not only the two-mile hike along the beach, but also the prospect of a swim in the ocean in his animal form. Gerard shared his psyche with a weedy sea dragon, so he could get away with shifting just about anywhere.

"Hey, what do you think's going on?"

Following where Kyger pointed, Gerard spotted Enforcer Dare urging a brawny auburn-haired stranger toward the largest condominium. He knew the place housed Alpha Kaiser's offices as well as security. With the way Dare held the stranger, Gerard figured he was a trespasser.

Except, that wasn't why Gerard felt his heartrate spike. The winds changed direction, and the stranger's scent hit his senses like a one-two punch. His mouth watered with a need to taste, and his dick thickened behind his shorts.

Gerard even felt his fingers twitch, and he wondered what those red and brown locks would feel like sliding through his fingers.

"You okay, Gerard?" Kyger asked, squeezing his upper arm. "You know him?"

Shaking his head, Gerard started moving forward at a fast clip. "Nope. Not yet." He cast a quick glance Kyger's way and gave his buddy a wide grin as excitement coursed through him. "But I will soon. That's my mate!"

CHAPTER TWO

*W*ell, *I found Price, and I didn't even need to ask Graham for help.*

Except, holy hell. What kind of rabbit hole did I fall into?

From noticing Price's lack of aging, then finding out that he always falsified his blood tests, Britt had already wrapped his brain around the idea of vampires. He figured accepting shapeshifters shouldn't be so hard, right? After all, werewolf stories had to come from somewhere.

Didn't they?

Britt didn't resist when a huge black man, who was evidently Price's boyfriend—*perhaps partner, husband, or significant other, I'm not sure what they're called these days*—continued to grip his upper arm and urge him toward the double glass doors of the largest condominium structure. He appreciated that Price had vouched for him to his man. Otherwise, Britt wasn't certain what the big lug would have attempted to do to him.

Maybe drown me in the ocean to hide their secret?

Hiking along the shoals toward the *World of Aquatica* housing units, Britt had been damn near shocked out of his mind to spot Price. Well, that hadn't been what surprised him. Instead, it was the fact that Price was dodging a massive gray tentacle, which extended from the ocean. The thing appeared to be attempting to swat him, and Price was hopping, twisting, and zipping to and fro at speeds Britt could barely follow.

Yep. Vampire.

Without thought, Britt had pulled his *Glock* and begun

shooting. An inhuman roar had rolled in from the direction of the ocean, carried easily over the crashing of the waves on the surf. Several more tentacles had instantly risen from the depths and grabbed Britt.

Britt had been disarmed embarrassingly fast, but really, what did one expect against giant octopus tentacles controlled by a sentient being?

Not that I would ever have guessed that at the time.

Price had come racing toward him, but instead of attacking the beast, he'd started to . . . talk to it. From his words, Britt had realized the man was reasoning with the creature.

"Dare, come on, beloved," Price had cried. "It was just a misunderstanding." He had his hands lifted in placation, and he stood under one of the tentacles holding Britt aloft. Price stared out to sea as he continued, "This is Britt. I've mentioned him before. He thought I was in danger and was trying to help." Finally, Price had peered up at Britt. "Right?"

"Y-Yeah," Britt had confirmed roughly, barely able to breathe around the tight squeeze of the tentacle holding him. "Shit, man. What the fuck?"

"Put Britt down, Dare," Price had encouraged, waving toward the beach. "Then come meet him. He already knows I'm something other. It's safe."

To Britt's shock, the tentacles had lowered him to the beach. A second later, they'd released him and slithered back into the water, disappearing beneath the waves.

"What the hell, Price?" Britt had cried, glancing from his friend to the water and back again. He couldn't help backing up a couple of steps or the fact that fear continued to pump adrenaline through him, urging him to flee. "What's going on?"

"I should ask you the same thing, Britt," Price had countered. Waving toward him, he cocked his head. "What are you doing here?" Then a huge, dark-skinned bruiser had come stalking out of the water, as naked as the day he was born. His expression had appeared thunderous even as Price growled and grabbed a towel and a pair of shorts off of a nearby rock. "Damn." He'd handed the items to the guy. "Sorry, Dare. Looks like we have a lot of explaining to do."

Britt had thought he was trying to save his friend. Instead, he learned he'd been shooting at his buddy's lover.

Holy Christ on a cracker!

Welcome to the rabbit hole, Alice.

Britt didn't know if it was shock or what, but he continued to move placidly within Dare's grip. Price had called ahead to a man he called Alpha Kaiser. From Britt's research, he knew that Kaiser Roush was one of the co-owners of the place. He shared the business with his brother, William Roush.

After a perfunctory knock on a door, Dare opened it and pushed Britt forward.

Britt found himself in a nicely appointed lounging room. There were several comfortable-looking leather sofas, a couple of chairs, and several end tables. A sideboard stood along one wall with a number of decanters and carafes resting upon it. A couple of mini-fridges were positioned underneath. There was even a flatscreen TV hanging on another wall. Although, at that second, it was off.

The imposing figure seated in one of the leather chairs drew Britt's attention. He had the sudden urge to stand up straight and salute — something he hadn't done in nearly ten years. The man's piercing green eyes held an intensity that screamed in-charge, alpha male.

Britt didn't even need to be introduced.

This is Kaiser Roush.

Kaiser arched one black brow as he swept his gaze over Britt. For a few seconds, he didn't say anything. Then Kaiser took a sip of whatever was in his tumbler.

Judging by the amber color, Britt would guess whiskey.

Before Britt could decide if he was supposed to apologize, Kaiser moved his attention to Price. "So . . . this is the army friend who warned you about the military police?"

Price nodded once. "Yes, Alpha. This is Britt O'Connor." After a second of hesitation, he added, "We worked together on a number of missions over our years in the military together."

Kaiser returned his attention back to Britt. "And he showed up on the beach and shot at Dare."

Wincing, Britt lifted both hands. "That was a misunderstanding," he hurried to cut in. When Kaiser arched one brow in silent question, he quickly added, "I thought Dare's, uh, octopus was attacking Price." Britt rubbed the back of his neck uneasily before admitting, "Uh, I mean, I get that Price is something else. Vampire, probably." *Good god. Did I just put that out there?* "But I didn't know about your kind existing."

As Kaiser hummed, his expression turned speculative. "If you were only here looking for Price, then why didn't you just call him or buzz at the gate?"

Grimacing, Britt admitted, "I'm on the run."

Kaiser sighed deeply. "Of course, you are." A muscle ticked in the big man's jaw once, twice. Then he asked, "Government, military, or other?"

Britt felt a flutter in his gut, not understanding that response in the slightest.

"Alpha Kaiser's in a meeting, Gerard," Head Enforcer Eban stated from where he was seated on a comfortable sofa. He had his feet crossed before him and had lowered the book he'd been reading to his thigh.

As far as Gerard knew, Eban was one of the few — if any — people in the area who still insisted on reading everything in print. The great white shark shifter didn't care for technology. It was only since he'd mated with the human retired Navy SEAL that Eban had agreed to always carry a cell phone with him.

Gerard had nearly fallen off his chair in surprise when he'd heard that. Except, a second later, it'd made sense to him. Mates could get a shifter to do damn near anything . . . including tolerate something they hated.

In Eban's words, that would be new-fangled technology.

"I know the alpha's in a meeting," Gerard declared, leading the way into the room. Kyger followed, probably to offer moral support. As much as it galled him to do so—he would much rather burst into the room, after all—Gerard took a seat in a chair in the sitting room that acted as Alpha Kaiser's outer office. When Kyger sat down near him and Eban arched a brow while giving him a questioning look, Gerard couldn't help but blurt out, "The alpha's meeting with my mate."

Eban's brown brows shot up. "Britt O'Connor is your mate?" he asked incredulously. With a shake of his head that betrayed his disbelief as surely as his scent did, he demanded, "How do you even know him?" Eban's eyes narrowed, and his gaze turned accusatory. "When'd you meet him, and why haven't you mentioned this before?"

Shaking his head quickly, Gerard told him, "I haven't officially met him." When Eban's expression took on a hint of confusion, he pointed toward the hallway he'd just entered through. "I was on my way to change before a hike and got a whiff of his scent." With his excitement surging anew, Gerard grinned broadly. "Just like you and others have said, the sensation's indescribable." With a sigh of anticipation, he wondered what kind of man his mate—*Britt O'Connor, what a strong name*—would be like. "He's mine."

Blowing out a breath, Eban rose to his feet. "I need to report this to Alpha Kaiser," he declared. With a shake of his head, he muttered, "He's supposed to be a friend of Price's, but he ended up shooting at Dare."

Gerard gaped as he watched Eban tap his knuckles against

the door twice before gripping the knob. Rising to his feet, he couldn't control the way his heartrate began to accelerate. Gerard even took a step toward his alpha's study.

Eban opened the door halfway and stuck his head into the opening. "Alpha Kaiser, I apologize for the interruption."

"It's fine, Enforcer Eban." Alpha Kaiser's voice came from within. "After you tell me the issue, please notify Ovram that I need to see him immediately."

"Of course, Alpha," Eban replied instantly. "I'll contact him. Except, uh—" He seemed to hesitate, his head turning as if he were looking around the room.

"Spit it out, Eban." Alpha Kaiser sounded amused.

Gerard hoped that meant the meeting was going fairly well. He mentally cringed as he recalled Eban saying that his mate had attacked Dare. Considering the shifter was a giant octopus, Gerard couldn't imagine why the man would do such a thing.

Must be a story there.

"Uh, Alpha Kaiser, Gerard is here," Eban replied slowly. He scrubbed a hand through his dark-brown hair as he stated, "He caught Britt's scent when he was on his way in, and he's, uh"—Eban heaved a put-upon sigh, then blurted out—"he's under the impression that Britt is his mate."

For several long seconds—seconds where sweat popped out on Gerard's temples—Alpha Kaiser didn't respond. Then a deep, "Really?" came from within.

"Really, Alpha." Eban glanced over his shoulder at him, and Gerard nodded quickly, before refocusing within. "He's pretty adamant."

"Hmmm." The low sound was followed by a deep, husky chuckle. "Excellent. Show him in."

When Eban turned back and faced Gerard, if someone had knocked him over with a feather, Gerard figured that was the expression Eban would have sported.

Beyond shocked.

Gerard couldn't help but take a step forward, eager to meet the delicious-smelling man inside the next room. Butterflies bumped in his belly, and he shifted from foot to foot. Anticipation even caused heat to flood through his veins.

"Well, head on in," Eban urged, stepping backward. As he moved, he swung the door open wider. The head enforcer's attention had already turned toward the room again. "I'll find a security replacement for Ovram so we can get him over here."

"Good," Alpha Kaiser responded.

As Gerard slowly took a step forward, then another, his palms began to sweat. The hairs on his arms stood on end. A shiver swept up his spine.

Gods, my mate is in there.

"You okay?"

Gerard turned, finding Kyger standing at his side. He touched his shoulder lightly. His smile turned from concern to warm and reassuring.

"Head on in, man," Kyger urged, squeezing his shoulder. "And congrats."

Taking in a deep breath, Gerard nodded once. He knew the second he stepped inside that door, his life would change. Then he realized that wasn't actually true.

My life has already changed.

After clasping Kyger's hand where it rested on his shoulder, Gerard murmured, "Thanks. I'll catch ya later. Okay?"

Kyger smiled as he drew away from him. "Can't wait to meet him, man." Lifting his hand to the side of his face in a *call me* gesture, he ordered, "Find out what his favorite pizza and beer is. I'll drop it off so ya don't have to worry about cookin'."

"You rock, Kyger." Lifting his fist, Gerard grinned when his fellow shifter bumped it. "Talk to ya in a bit."

With a jaunty grin, a wave, and a wink, Kyger turned away and headed out of the room.

Turning away from where his friend was leaving, Gerard blew out a sharp breath. He did his best to appear confident as he strode past Eban and into the room. When Gerard entered, he couldn't help but pause as his gaze fell on the stranger in the room — Britt O'Connor.

Gerard's blood rushed south from just the man's handsome features. While obviously older — perhaps in his mid-fifties — he sported smooth-skinned, chiseled features. Gerard thought the scar running down Britt's face — from under his right ear to just under the edge of his jaw — made him appear distinguished.

Plus, when Gerard had been so far away outside and in the sunlight, he hadn't noticed the light salt and peppering in Britt's auburn hair. Now that he had, he couldn't help but think that the myriad of colors brought out the rich redness within his locks. Those same strands were tugged away from his handsome features in a loose ponytail. Gerard felt his fingers twitch as he was hit with a desire to cross the floor, sit next to the rugged man, and thread his fingers into the guy's hair.

With that desire raging through him, Gerard found himself moving slowly across the floor. He felt delight fill him to see Britt sitting, albeit stiffly, on a small sofa. Gerard strode purposefully to the guy's side and settled next to him.

Gerard began reaching for Britt's hair, completely entranced.

When Britt drew back, Gerard snapped out of it. He lowered his hand and straightened as he grimaced. Blowing out a breath, he shook his head sharply. Then Gerard forced a smile as he met Britt's wary green eyes.

"Sorry, Britt," Gerard rumbled with a deprecating laugh. "My mistake." Threading his fingers together in his lap, he glanced around the group, taking in their varying looks of amusement and understanding. Price smiled at him encouragingly, so Gerard returned his attention to Britt. Seeing the way the man's eyes were narrowed and how he was sweeping his gaze over him assessingly, Gerard grinned rakishly. "Can't help it. You're a handsome fella, and the minute I spotted ya, I knew I hadta meet ya."

That's reasonably close to the truth, right? After all, even if he's a friend of Price, he probably doesn't know about paranormals.

CHAPTER THREE

Britt glanced over his shoulder at Gerard before returning his attention to Ovram's sweet computer set-up. He did his best to focus on something he understood—delving into cyberspace for information. Britt certainly didn't want to think about the load of crazy Price and his friends had dumped on him.

Except, with Gerard remaining in the room, Britt was having a tough time doing that. Britt had accepted his bisexuality decades before, so the fact that Gerard was a man wasn't the issue. He'd never discriminated with his partners on the rare occasion when he went out to scratch that itch. Britt cared only about the sex of his one-night stand insomuch as to be able to please the other person.

Britt had never met anyone who'd interested him for more than one night. While deployed, that had been a good thing. He'd watched way too many couples break up due to the stress of long distance, lack of communication, and misunderstandings.

Then, when Britt had gotten out and gone into private work, he still hadn't been interested. He'd figured it was because he was too jaded. Britt also thought he was a bit selfish with his space, considering he'd made himself a mountain retreat and had never invited a trick there. That required a level of trust Britt didn't think he had anymore.

And these guys think that just because of some weird fated mate-pull shit, I'm going to accept a relationship with some guy I just met.

"What do you like on your pizza, Britt?"

Gerard rested his hand on Britt's shoulder, drawing his attention. The move also caused the hairs on his arm to stand on end and the heat of arousal to simmer through his body. Britt barely repressed a shiver as he felt the touch all the way down to his toes.

Holy shit! Is that what that expression means?

Peering down at him with a wide smile, Gerard looked devastatingly handsome as he held up the cell phone in his other hand. "Got my buddy, Kyger, on the line, and he's gonna bring us pizza," he told him. "That way, ya can keep workin', but ya won't starve."

Even as Britt nodded, trying to find his tongue, something else clicked in his brain. A shifter was instinct-driven to see to the needs of their mate. Feeding him was Gerard's way of taking care of him.

Britt had been self-sufficient since the day he joined the army at eighteen, fresh out of foster care. Hell, even before that, he took care of himself. While he'd never suffered the abuse while in the system that he'd heard horror stories about, the group homes he'd lived at had been busy and crowded, leaving him to his own devices much of the time. Fortunately, they'd provided computers. Alone often, Britt had used the time to develop his skills.

Britt's stomach growling reminded him that he was hungry.

Meeting Gerard's expectant gaze, Britt answered, "Pretty much anything. Extra cheese. No pineapple."

"Not a fan of pineapple, aye?" Gerard lifted his phone to his ear and asked, "Ya get that?" As Britt recalled being told about shifters' exceptional hearing, Gerard added, "Great, man. I appreciate it. Yep, I'll introduce ya when ya bring it in a bit." Then Gerard disconnected the call and refocused on Britt. "Don't like the taste or consistency?"

Gerard slipped his phone into his shorts' pocket before easing onto the chair next to Britt. He slid his hand down Britt's arm to land on his wrist. The glide of the other man's callouses on his flesh caused goose bumps to rise on Britt.

And why aren't I pulling away?

Except, Britt found his hand frozen on the keyboard. He wasn't even typing anymore. Britt heard Ovram clicking the keys of his own keyboard a few feet away, but Britt couldn't seem to get his brain to focus on work.

Instead, Britt found himself sharing, "I don't really recall what pineapple tastes like or what it feels like on my tongue. I'm allergic. Like, *really* allergic." The fact that pineapple hadn't been a part of military rations had been a fantastic thing.

Gerard's warm blue eyes widened, and his lips parted in a silent *oh*. The move drew Britt's attention to the man's mouth, and he found himself wondering what the shifter tasted like. Britt hadn't bothered kissing a male hook-up in . . . he couldn't remember when, but he barely resisted the urge to lean forward and do it right then.

"Well, damn," Gerard murmured, shaking his head a little. "I'll remember that." With a squeeze to Britt's wrist, the shifter added, "Thanks for tellin' me. I happen to like pineapple, so I know there's some in my kitchen. I'll toss it, though."

"I don't care if other people eat it," Britt countered, yanking his attention away from Gerard's delectable mouth. *Shit! Did I just think that?* Britt cleared his throat, wishing he could clear his brain just as easily. "I know how to be careful."

After all, Britt had been living with the knowledge his whole life.

Gerard shook his head. "Naw, never want to run the risk of pineapple juice gettin' on your food by accident. Better to be safe," he stated decisively. "Do ya carry an *Epi-Pen* or somethin' like that?" Cocking his head, Gerard continued absently, "Maybe we should have Doc Anthony draw your blood before we bond. That way, he can compare it afterward and see if anythin' changes." Gerard grinned rakishly as he openly continued, "Humans get a few perks after bondin' with a shifter, after all." With a wink, he added, "Maybe no longer bein' allergic will be one of 'em for ya."

"You're just assuming I'm going to accept all this fated mate bullshit and bond with you," Britt grumbled gruffly, clenching his hands into fists. "Why? You don't know any-thing about me."

"Doesn't matter, Britt," Ovram cut in, revealing that he'd been listening even as he continued to work. "Fate's timing is always impeccable, and I haven't seen a couple not work out, yet." Cutting a glance their way, Ovram shrugged as he con-tinued, "Doesn't mean it doesn't take work, just like any rela-tionship, but the benefits far outweigh any cons." The shifter returned his attention to his monitor as he snorted. "Besides, the Fates like to get their way, and they make it damn uncom-fortable for anyone to try walking away from their mate, even the human side who doesn't recognize the pull for what it is."

"What's that supposed to mean?" Britt demanded.

Price looked up from the tablet he'd been reading. "It means you'd probably end up with a hell of a lot of longing and maybe some wet dreams." Grinning widely, showing off his fangs, he waggled his eyebrows. "Why bother going through that when you can have the real thing right up front?"

"Wet dreams?" Britt muttered incredulously. "What the hell?"

With a shrug, Price sobered. "Like Ovram said. The Fates like to get their way." Then he showed something on his screen to Dare, who was sitting next to him. "You want one of these for Christmas?"

Dare growled softly as he peered at whatever Price was showing him. His expression grew heated as he focused on his lover. "Oh, that would be so much fun, my vampire," he rumbled. Threading his big fingers through Price's hair, Dare cupped the man's nape. "I love the way you think."

Then Dare drew a softly chuckling Price into a deep kiss.

Britt returned his attention to his laptop, feeling the heat of embarrassment threatening at the base of his neck. He'd worked with Price many times over their years in the military together. They'd even gone bar hopping a time or two. Britt had *never* seen the man so openly expressive of his desire before.

Feeling Gerard squeeze his wrist and hearing him murmur, "Ya'll get used to it. We're a touchy-feely lot when it comes to our mates."

"Touchy-feely," Britt mused softly, his gaze lowering to where Gerard continued to hold his wrist. "Is that why?" He tipped his chin, indicating where the shifter touched him.

"Yep." Gerard squeezed him lightly. "Can't help it, and don't really wanna try. Hope ya don't mind."

Do I mind? Do I care that Gerard is sitting next to me and touching me?

To Britt's surprise, he didn't. *Still.* "No, I don't mind. That still doesn't mean I'm agreeing to bonding," he warned, frowning at the handsome, grinning blond. "I've never been in a relationship, and I've been called a selfish bastard by others on more than one occasion."

Normally, it was by a trick that wanted a repeat, but Britt refused to give them his phone number.

Gerard didn't seem to be put off. "That's okay. Me neither." Still smiling widely, showing off even white teeth, he claimed, "We'll figure it out together."

Before Britt could comment on that, Ovram called his name. "Do you recognize this guy?"

Britt turned his attention to Ovram's screen. He took in the picture of the man in a dark outfit, and something niggled in the back of his mind. Britt thought he should know him.

"He looks familiar," Britt admitted, frowning. "But I can't place him."

Gerard took in Britt's frustrated expression. His mate obviously must have thought he should know the guy. Gerard wished he could come up with some way to ease his frustration.

Wait, I know just the thing.

Rising from his seat, Gerard moved behind Britt. When he rested his hands on his mate's shoulders, he felt him tense. Gently, Gerard dug his fingers into the tight muscles there.

As Gerard began a light massage, he crooned, "Relax, my mate." He couldn't help vocally claiming the man, reminding him of what they were to each other. His mate's delicious, masculine aroma in his nostrils made thinking of anything other than touching and exploring the handsome human difficult. "We'll figure this out. My pod-mates are fantastic at this sort of thing."

Gerard had watched his people clean up the messes surrounding many newly mated couples. He firmly believed that Fate brought people together when one of them was in need of the support of the other. While Gerard didn't know much about computers like Ovram, he knew he could help in other ways.

Britt growled softly even as he began to relax. "You like calling me that," he grumbled, sounding a mix of irritated and frustrated.

Gerard would have been worried, but he smelled a little bit of amusement in Britt's scent, too.

"Yep," Gerard decided to go with. "Been waitin' for this day for longer than ya've been alive, Britt." Leaning down, he gave in to his basest of instincts and nuzzled his nose against the side of Britt's neck. "Love the way ya smell." The allure of Britt's skin was too much, and Gerard slipped out his tongue and tasted him. When the slightly salty flavor burst across his taste buds, he groaned softly. "Taste delicious, too. Wanna lick ya all over."

Britt shivered under his ministrations.

Gerard could smell Britt's arousal, musky and deep. His mate was doing his damnedest to ignore their connection, and Gerard wasn't going to allow him to do that for long. As much as his instincts urged him to give his mate whatever he wanted, that didn't include allowing the handsome human to ignore their connection.

"Are you trying to seduce me while in a room full of people?" Britt asked gruffly, a bit of tension returning to his shoulders. "Because I don't do exhibitionism."

"Good to know, Britt," Gerard replied nonchalantly, keeping his tone even and relaxed. "Gotta admit, in the past, I hadn't really cared if anyone saw me while gettin' it on, but I've never done anythin' in public." As Gerard thought about his past, he knew he would always be careful in the future. "With you, though" — he couldn't help the growl that entered his words as he finished — "no one's gonna see ya but me from now on. I ain't sharin'."

"Wow," Britt muttered under his breath. "Shifters are possessive." Frowning over his shoulder, he stated gruffly, "I've never met a man that has interested me for more than one night." Britt hesitated a second, then added, "Or a woman, for that matter."

Gerard got it. His mate was trying to warn him away, warn him that he wasn't a good bet. All his words achieved, however, was to fill him with a rush of pleasure — because, in an odd way, Britt was expressing concern for Gerard — as well as a healthy dose of jealousy.

"You'll see how that'll change, Britt," Gerard countered softly, continuing with his massage. After a few heartbeats of hesitation, where Gerard struggled with what else to say as he worked the hard muscles of the broad-shouldered man seated before him, he tried another tactic to connect. "Where do ya call home?" he asked curiously. "Got any family left there?"

Britt scoffed, shaking his head. "No family. Grew up in group homes before joining the military at eighteen." With a hum, he murmured, "Built myself a real nice retreat on several hundred acres that backs up to privately owned logging country." His voice turned appreciative as he stated, "Just me, the wildlife, and my computers." Britt growled as he finished, "Until this shit with whoever these assholes are. Seems no matter how many I help others take down, more just pop up in their place." Cracking his knuckles, he grumbled, "Once we figure out who they are, they're gonna learn they messed with the wrong recluse."

"Yes, we will," Gerard agreed as another piece of the puzzle that was his mate fell into place. His mate was jaded, and he'd obviously cut himself off from the main world. Gerard needed to help him learn to connect, especially with himself. "So, you were in the military with Price, right?"

Britt grunted in confirmation.

Gerard didn't mind his taciturn responses. "You a SEAL like him?"

Nodding, Britt told him, "I am."

"So a highly trained soldier, then," Gerard mused. Applying light pressure to a knot near Britt's shoulder blade, he commented, "You know how to scuba dive?"

Turning his head a smidge, Britt eyed him over his shoulder. "Of course."

Grinning, Gerard urged, "Come with me after pizza. I wanna show ya a different kind of wildlife."

Britt hesitated, and for an instant, Gerard feared he would say no.

"You may as well, Britt," Ovram encouraged, earning

Gerard's gratitude. "I've loaded the picture into my facial recognition program. He was leading the group who broke into your house." Relaxing back in his seat, Ovram crossed his arms over his chest. "We can't move forward until I get a hit. It could take an hour, or it could take all night. Take the time to relax while you can."

To Gerard's relief, Britt only hesitated a moment more before nodding. "Okay." Squinting up at him, he asked, "What do you want to show me?"

Gerard grinned again. "A whole new world."

CHAPTER FOUR

Britt couldn't understand for the life of him why he'd agreed to go scuba diving with Gerard. Sure, it'd been years, and he worried he would be a little rusty at it, but it wasn't his pride that had urged him forward. No, maybe it was the challenge of it.

In the past, Britt had learned to scuba dive in the military. Having the ability had opened doors. He'd been able to expand his horizons.

Plus, Britt had found it enjoyable, even though he'd only managed to do it for fun a handful of times.

That must be why I agreed. I haven't done it in years, and I recall it being fun.

Either way, Britt would never back out. He said he would do it, and so he would.

Standing in a locker room full of supplies, Britt watched as Gerard located a wet suit, flippers, and goggles in his size. "Put those on while I gather your tanks and respirator and shit." Then Gerard took a step backward and paused, looking uncertain. "You, uh"—he rubbed the back of his neck with one hand, and his voice deepened—"ya need a hand gettin' that on?"

"I can manage," Britt replied gruffly. "It hasn't been *that* long."

Gerard offered a roguish grin. "Yeah, but it woulda let me see ya naked."

Britt gaped.

Before he'd managed to gather himself enough to respond,

Gerard chuckled as he swept his gaze over Britt's body in blatant interest. Then he gave a jaunty wave as he turned and sauntered out of the room.

Britt couldn't help the way his attention fell to Gerard's departing ass. The slender male had a great ass, after all. As much as Britt wanted to deny it, he never lied to himself.

I want in that ass.

Except, Britt knew that fucking Gerard would open up a whole new can of worms. The man would think it was him accepting their whole paranormal partnership thing. While Britt wanted the man, he couldn't fathom still wanting him the next morning.

It had never happened before.

He couldn't imagine it happening now — paranormal shit or not.

Fortunately, with Gerard gone, Britt's line of thinking killed his burgeoning erection. Putting on a wetsuit with a boner would have been hell. That was what he'd heard anyway, having never experienced it himself.

Britt quickly stripped, folding his clothes and setting them on the bench. Just as he'd slipped his arms into the suit and begun to reach behind himself for the cord attached to the zipper, he heard his phone ring. Freezing, Britt stared at his jacket, where he'd left it in the pocket.

I thought I'd turned it off.

Frowning, Britt reached beneath the folds and retrieved the ringing device. He saw his boss's name come up on the screen — Lucas Derringer — and grimaced. Britt hadn't logged into work in several days, since he'd been on the run, and he hadn't taken the time to find out if those he reported to at work could be trusted.

If I don't answer, I'm pretty sure I'm fired. What to do, what to do . . .

After letting out a sigh, Britt answered the call. "This is Britt."

"Britt, Lucas here," Lucas stated by way of greeting. "You haven't responded to my last three emails. What's up?"

"I had an emergency," Britt stated evasively. "I was called out of state, so I don't have my equipment with me."

Not that that same equipment had kept him safe. Someone, somewhere, had cracked his safeguards. He really wanted to know who, and he hoped Ovram would be able to figure it out.

Shit. I should be with the shifter, trying to figure out if my worm worked, not getting ready to go swimming.

"Family emergency?" Lucas questioned. "I didn't realize you still had any."

Britt narrowed his eyes, distrust slithering through him. He couldn't ever recall discussing the fact that he'd been a foster kid with Lucas or anyone from the firm, for that matter. Britt worked behind the scenes for them, keeping their security forces safe. He rarely actually interacted with anyone other than Lucas and a handful of team leaders.

"I don't," Britt replied slowly. "Different kind of family."

"Different kind?" Lucas pressed. "What's going on? Where are you?"

"I'm sorry, Lucas," Britt replied, deciding it was time to shut down the conversation. A sixth sense he always listened to was telling him something hinky was going on. "I need to go. Either list me on vacation, paid or unpaid, whichever, or fire my ass."

As Britt lowered his phone from his ear, his finger hovering over the disconnect button, he heard Lucas snap, "What the hell, Britt. I oughta fire you just for talking to me like that." Britt hesitated, continuing to listen. "But you're too good to fire just for that." Lucas heaved a sigh through the line before demanding, "Just tell me if you're even in the country so I can list it on your leave of absence paperwork. That'll be good enough."

Britt opened his mouth, then closed it again, distrust still burning within him. Staring at the bank of lockers, he struggled with what to do.

When Britt felt warm hands rest on his bare back, he cursed and jolted forward. He banged his hand on the open locker door and dropped his phone. Whirling, Britt found Gerard standing there wearing a lopsided smile while holding his hands up in placation.

"Sorry," Gerard murmured, his Australian accent thick with appreciation. "Saw your suit hadn't been done up and couldn't resist all that skin." With a wink, he reached for him again. "Why doncha let me zip ya up? Then ya can get your phone."

Sucking in a deep breath, Britt slowly turned. He didn't think Gerard needed to do quite so much sliding of his hands over his skin as he zipped up his wetsuit, but he couldn't deny how great it felt. By the time Gerard had tugged the zipper into position at his nape, Britt could barely take a full breath.

Wonderful. Now I'm going to be scuba diving with a boner, after all.

Seeing the top of Britt's ass crack on display because his wet suit wasn't zipped had driven every logical thought right out of Gerard's brain. He'd needed to touch all that smooth, tanned flesh more than his next breath. Having his mate give in and let him actually zipper him, well . . . he appreciated that he wasn't the one wearing a wetsuit because he was hard as nails behind the fly of his shorts.

"Thanks," Britt stated gruffly. Then he crouched and located his phone. Lifting it, he revealed the cracked, blank screen. "Oh well." Then Britt tossed the phone onto the pile of clothes he'd placed in a locker.

"Sorry about that," Gerard offered with a wince. "I'll get ya a replacement."

Britt shrugged. "Don't worry about it. I'd been using a

burner for the last several days." He frowned at the device before admitting, "I turned that one off before leaving home. Must have bumped it at some point for it to turn back on."

Gerard noticed that he didn't sound too certain about that, but he didn't know Britt well enough to question it.

Britt closed the locker and peered at the gear Gerard had left on another bench. As he began picking it up, he glanced Gerard's way. "What about you?"

Grinning, Gerard shook his head. "Sea animal shifter, remember? I can breathe underwater."

"Right," Britt whispered. "Still getting used to that." After slinging the air tanks over his shoulders, he asked, "So, uh, what animal do you, um . . . you guys called it sharing your psyche with?"

"Oh, right." Gerard picked up a few items to help and began leading the way toward the elevator. "I'm a weedy sea dragon."

"Uhhhhh, I don't think I know what that is," Britt admitted, following him without question.

"Well, I'm a fish that's similar to a seahorse," Gerard explained, pushing the down button. "Most of us are native to part of the waters around Australia." When the carriage opened, Gerard led the way inside. "Our tail isn't prehensile, like a seahorse, though, so we can't hang onto stuff. Instead, we have these leaf-like growths on our body that look like weeds and help us blend into the seaweed beds, which is our natural habitat."

"A seahorse," Britt mused, drawing his brows together thoughtfully. "Male seahorses carry the fertilized eggs, if I remember correctly." When Gerard nodded, confirming his statement, Britt asked, "You said your animal is similar to them. Do sea dragons do that, too? The male carries the eggs?"

"Ah, yeah." Britt chuckled, feeling his cheeks heat a little.

"But I don't think I can get pregnant in human form."

"Don't *think*?" Gerard gaped at him. "Uh, that hadn't even crossed my mind." He stared at him with shock in his wide green eyes. "You don't *know*?"

"Well." Gerard rubbed the back of his neck as he shifted from foot to foot in discomfort. "I've had other paranormals fuck me bare on occasion, not worryin' about disease and all, and they've never knocked me up." With a shrug, Gerard muttered, "And weedy sea dragon shifters are one of the few races that are born in animal form, and we almost immediately go our separate ways from our parents." Feeling his cheeks heat with a blush, he swallowed as he admitted, "I was caught as a hatchling and lived for a year in the aquarium of a seafood restaurant. A dingo shifter recognized me as a fellow shifter, broke into the restaurant one night, and rescued me." The elevator stopped moving, and the doors began to open. "Anyway, the dingo taught me how to be human, and seventy years later, I moved to the Americas to work for Alpha Kaiser."

"Holy shit," Britt rumbled. Staring at him in clear disbelief, he swept his gaze up and down Gerard's body. His attention snagged at Gerard's crotch for an instant before he must have caught himself, for he once again met his gaze when he asked, "Just how old are you?"

Appreciating that Britt appeared to like how he looked, Gerard grinned at him. "Well, I don't know my exact birthdate, but I'll be seventy-eight next spring."

"Wow." Britt scoffed. "You age well. You don't look a day over—" Turning toward the exit, Britt's words were cut off on a whistle. He exited the elevator car and stood on the platform affixed sixty feet above the underground cavern's floor below. "Holy shit. I never would have expected this place," Britt whispered. "I thought you were taking me to a dock or something."

Gerard panned over the expansive room, taking it all in. The massive cavern sported a one-hundred-plus-foot ceiling and a large lake. A metal stairway had been bolted into the cavern's side and led the way to a sandy beach. There were sconces drilled into the walls at various locations and heights, offering a romantic ambiance.

It was also a fantastic place to take a nap, and Gerard had dozed in the waters on more than one occasion.

"Come on," Gerard urged, placing his palm on the small of Britt's back. "Let's go enjoy the water."

As Britt started moving, he asked, "Why doesn't the elevator go all the way to the bottom?"

"This cavern floods during heavy storms," Gerard explained, descending the stairs. "There's even been a time or two where water's filled a bit of the elevator shaft."

"Damn."

Gerard nodded as he pinned a serious look on Britt. "Please don't ever try comin' down here durin' a storm."

Britt's brows shot up, and he paused near the bottom of the stairs. "I would never put myself in unnecessary harm."

Knowing that was probably the best promise he was likely to get from a SEAL, Gerard nodded. "Thanks, mate." He spotted the way Britt's green eyes narrowed just a smidge, so before his human could say anything, Gerard waggled his eyebrows and teased, "Come on, SEAL. Let's go get wet."

To Gerard's pleasure, the corners of Britt's lips twitched a little.

Good. My serious mate does have some sense of humor.

Leading the way toward where the waves lapped just a little at the sand, Gerard told him, "There's a tunnel that leads to the ocean." He pointed toward the side. "Right now, it's totally underwater." Gerard paused, gripping the hem of his shirt. "You okay in tight spaces?"

Probably should have checked that before.

"Yeah, no problem," Britt told him as he began double-checking everything before donning the equipment. Glancing toward Gerard, Britt asked, "Did you grab a spear gun or something?"

"Spear gun?" Gerard wasn't following. "Why?"

"If we're going into the ocean, we should have a way to protect ourselves," Britt stated, buckling the last clasp and pinning his gaze on him. "What if we get attacked by a shark or something?"

Gerard grinned as he pointed toward the water. "No need to worry. We already have protection." Pausing, he whipped his shirt over his head, hearing a gasp before his head emerged again. Seeing what had caught Britt's attention—a very large dorsal fin—Gerard gripped the bigger man's upper arm and squeezed lightly. "That's Eban. He introduced ya to Ovram, remember? He's goin'ta be accompanyin' us, and he's a great white shark."

Even though Gerard knew the information had already been given to Britt, he still reminded him, "We're totally cognizant in animal form. Eban won't hurt us, even as his shark." With a shrug, he stated, "He's here to protect us. So's Craeg. He's a minke whale shifter. My guess is he's waitin' outside the grotto for us."

Gerard didn't add that the pair were there to make certain Britt didn't wander off, either. The human was probably still in shock from their information dump.

And here I am, about to show him something else shocking . . . me shifting.

Pushing that thought out of his mind when he saw a still-gaping Britt nodding, Gerard gripped the button of his khaki shorts. He quickly opened them and pushed them down. He couldn't do anything about his raging erection, and he didn't bother trying to hide it, either.

Gerard mentally preened when he saw the way Britt was eyeing him. Appreciation lit the larger man's deep green eyes. For a few seconds, Britt's focus landed on Gerard's cock, and his nostrils flared while his face flushed.

Then Britt turned his attention to the water.

After forcing back a goofy grin, Gerard toed off his boots and socks. Then he sauntered toward the water. Feeling the hairs on his nape stand on end, he just knew if he turned around, he would see Britt watching him.

Gerard resisted and waded into the water. At least the cold helped with his erection, causing him to soften nearly to half-mast. Once chest-deep in water, Gerard turned to face Britt, pleased to find him only a few feet away.

"Okay. I'm going to shift now," Gerard warned his mate. "It'll only take a few seconds, and it doesn't hurt. I promise."

After watching Britt nod, despite the wariness in his expression, Gerard sank beneath the water and shifted.

CHAPTER FIVE

Britt expected the churning bubbles he recalled from when Dare had transformed. Except, that didn't happen. Instead, he didn't even see a ripple break the surface. Well, not that wasn't caused by the shark circling a couple of dozen yards away.

And isn't that a bizarre thought?

Curious, Britt settled his mask over his face and breathed, confirming everything was working. Then he eased under the surface. He peered through the water, surprised to see just how clear it was. The lights overhead illuminated everything just right so he could see at least twenty feet in every direction.

To his left, Britt found what he was looking for. He felt his heart rate spike as he tried to understand exactly what he was seeing. Gerard didn't look like Gerard anymore . . . but he wasn't an animal yet either. His body was going through a series of twists and contortions. Britt blinked a few times, doing his best to push down his shock.

Then . . . it was over . . . and something else floated where Gerard had once been.

Britt squinted at the small creature, knowing he'd never seen anything like it. The little animal floated toward him, and he stared in wonder. He could make out the head and body, and it did remind him of a seahorse. The body was a vibrant orange color, but just as Gerard had described, there were a number of odd seaweed-like appendages growing from his body in various shades of green.

As it drew closer, Britt was surprised by the mass of the thing. He figured it had to measure around fifty centimeters from the tip of its cylindrical snout to the end of its tail. The body was as big around as his fist and appeared to be covered in scale-like material.

Makes sense, him claiming to be a fish and all.

Recalling that shifters were sentient in animal form — *and this is Gerard* — Britt lifted a hand and reached for him. The sea dragon peered at him out of one black eye. Then it turned its head and stared at him with the other.

After a few seconds of perusal, the sea dragon swam closer to him. The beast rested its head against the back of Britt's crooked forefinger and nuzzled it. Accepting that as an invitation, Britt skimmed his fingertips down the side of the sea dragon's neck and body, then along one of the fronds. The scales felt smooth and cool against Britt's flesh, and he could just stare in amazement as his heart hammered in his chest.

I don't know how this is possible.

Just damn.

Gerard's sea dragon allowed Britt to explore him for a moment. Then the creature flicked its tail at his fingers and swam a few feet away. It turned back to look at Britt, and bubbles blew from the end of its snout.

Britt wondered if that was the sea dragon's way of teasing him. Still, he got the message. Swishing his flippers and angling his arms, he began swimming after the beast.

The sea dragon led the way through the water, and Britt noticed the rock wall closing in on his left. He realized they were entering the passageway, and he peered to the right. Britt could barely make out the other wall.

When Gerard had asked him if he had a problem with tight spaces, he'd thought the tunnel would be narrow, maybe even tough to get through. He realized now he'd been completely wrong. The tunnel had to be fifty feet across or more.

Spotting Eban's great white swimming ahead of them, Britt

realized that it made sense. Some of these shifters turned into really large animals. The shark had to be a good twenty-plus feet in length and five or six feet wide. While Britt hadn't seen the body of Dare's giant octopus, the length and thickness of the tentacles gave him some estimation.

Just huge.

When they exited the tunnel, Britt continued to follow. He noticed an animal off to the right that looked like a type of whale, although he couldn't identify the species. The mammal swam over to the great white and bumped its side before flanking him.

Okay. That has to be the other shifter Gerard mentioned – Craeg.

As Britt continued to swim, he panned his gaze over the sea bed. There were plenty of rock clusters interspersed along the sandy bottom. Occasionally, Britt caught movement out of the corner of his eye. When he turned to look, whatever it was had already disappeared.

Gerard's sea dragon must have noticed his interest. The little beast paused and followed his attention. It cocked its head as if studying the terrain.

With another blow of bubbles from his nose, the sea dragon glanced Britt's way before swishing off in that direction. Britt followed slowly, wondering what it was thinking. A second later, Gerard's beast disappeared into a crevice created by a pile of rocks.

Worry filled Britt, surprising him with its intensity.

Britt began to swim swiftly toward the rocks.

A flurry of gold and green-scaled fish erupted from the crack, making him pause. He watched the fish circle the area, darting this way and that, their scales reflecting off the tiny bit of sunlight that reached their depths. Gerard's sea dragon reappeared and swam with them for a moment, appearing to almost be dancing with them.

Smiling as he watched, Britt took in the show. He realized that was exactly what Gerard was doing for him. The beast before him wasn't actually an *it*. It was a *he*—Gerard—just in another form.

There was no way the sea dragon was trying to eat the fish, as half of them were as large or larger than himself. Instead, Gerard had urged the fish out of hiding for Britt's pleasure. He swam with them, helping them put on a show.

Just for me.

Something unfamiliar tightened in Britt's chest. His stomach even felt as if butterflies bumped within. He wanted to thank Gerard, but he knew now wasn't the time.

Britt would need to wait.

Gerard left the fish, and most of them swiftly returned to their hiding place. Gliding to his side, the sea dragon nuzzled the side of his neck not hidden by his mask. In return, Britt gently petted the beast in thanks.

Britt imagined the sea dragon had a pleased expression on its face.

That shouldn't be possible, but that's what it looks like.

Turning, Gerard led the way through the water once more. Interested in seeing what else the shifter wanted to show him, Britt quickly followed. They traveled along for several minutes before a deep trench opened before them, and Gerard led the way inside.

Britt stared in awe as a whole new world seemed to open before him. Beds of orange and green seaweed intermixed with interesting rock formations, probably caused by the shifting currents. Fish in various colors darted around the area.

Half-submerged in the sandy floor scooted a manta ray. A creature with a massive colorful shell clung to the rock wall with tentacles. While the five-foot shell reminded Britt of a snail, he knew they didn't have tentacles coming out the front.

When Gerard moved toward the large beast, Britt began swimming toward him, intending to intervene. The creature on the wall could easily use his tentacles to grab his sea dragon and probably hurt it.

Gerard must have noticed Britt's quick approach, for he paused and began floating toward him instead. Perhaps he recognized Britt's alarm, for he nuzzled into the side of his neck. Britt realized the move was to comfort him.

So very weird that I understand this . . . and it feels so damn good.

When Britt smiled once more and, using a cupped hand around Gerard's body to urge him away from the much larger animal, the sea dragon once again blew bubbles at him. Cocking his head, Britt eyed Gerard, wondering what was going on. He didn't stop the beast when it pulled away, although nerves fired through him when the sea dragon approached the large creature again . . . especially now that part of a head had emerged from the shell.

It was obviously watching them.

Gerard didn't seem at all concerned as it floated over to it. The sea dragon stopped on top of the beast's large curved shell. To Britt's amazement, the sea creature pushed off the wall, and using its tentacles, it began spinning and twirling, taking Gerard with him as if he were riding it.

Okaaaaaay. That must be a shifter. But what the hell is it?

When Gerard had seen Rawlins clinging to the rock wall, just finishing up a crustacean snack, he hadn't been able to resist going to the massive ammonite shifter. He figured Rawlins's human mate, Deckart, had to be working for him to be out swimming on his own. The large shifter was a friendly sort, and they'd played together on many occasions.

The fact that Britt had tried to intervene had absolutely tickled Gerard. He'd loved to see his human's protectiveness. He knew that Britt wanting to keep him safe was a great start to their relationship.

Although, I doubt he understands that yet.

Gerard wouldn't tell him, either. He knew Britt would need to come to these conclusions on his own. Even after only a few brief talks, he recognized the man's dominant personality and loner nature.

Britt thought he didn't need anyone. Before meeting Gerard, perhaps the human could have lived out the rest of his life by himself. Instead, the Fates had brought him to Gerard, and Gerard couldn't be happier about that.

I finally have my mate.

When Rawlins paused in his playful antics, Gerard took a few seconds to peer at Britt. He spotted the unmistakable curve of the man's lips behind his mask, revealing his amusement. The man's green eyes twinkled behind the plastic covering his face.

Deciding to try to get Britt in on the fun, Gerard tapped his snout against Rawlins's shell to get his attention. He eased his fins out of the ridges of Rawlins's shell, releasing his hold. Then he swam toward Britt. After whirling around his human's head a few times, Gerard started back toward Rawlins. He paused and looked back, making certain Britt was following.

He was, albeit slowly.

Gerard swam back to him, rounded him once, then returned to swimming toward Rawlins. To his pleasure, Britt seemed to get it, and he started swishing his flippers faster. Gerard stopped near Rawlins and tried to figure out how to convey his idea.

After a few seconds, Gerard sat on Rawlins's shell once more. Then he blew air through his snout, since Britt seemed to find the move amusing. His bid for attention worked. Except Britt shook his head.

Gerard returned to Britt's side. He bumped the back of his shoulder, urging him toward Rawlins again. After Britt had moved a few feet, Gerard swam back to Rawlins and resumed his perch.

Britt stared at him, stopping, perhaps not understanding. Then the human lifted both hands, palms out, even as he swam away a little.

Disappointment filled Gerard, and he wondered why his human would deny himself the joy and entertainment of riding an ammonite.

Does he still not understand?

Rawlins reached out with one tentacle and gripped Britt's leg, causing the human to freeze. His friend tugged his mate toward them. Using another couple of tentacles, Rawlins positioned his massive, five-foot shell against Britt's side.

Finally, Britt seemed to understand or maybe acquiesce. He wrapped his arms around Rawlins's shell. A few seconds later, he nodded that he was ready.

Digging his tentacles into the sand, Rawlins pushed off the ocean floor. If Gerard could have shouted with pleasure while in sea dragon form, he would have. In his animal form, he wasn't very fast. Mostly, his kind would drift along a seaweed bed in search of small crustaceans or zooplankton. Gerard imagined flying through the water on Rawlins's back was as close to racing through the waves as he would get.

A short time later, Rawlins reached the top of the trench. He continued to whirl and circle, but his movements took them closer and closer to the tunnel and grotto. When they reached the underground lake, Gerard knew the ride was over. He released his hold, and Britt did the same, following his actions.

Rawlins swam a few yards away, moving toward the surface, and began to shift.

Bumping Britt's shoulder, Gerard encouraged his mate to turn away from the sight before he could get an eyeful. Shifters weren't shy by nature, and their nudity had never bothered him before. With his mate in the water with them, however, Gerard felt a deep well of jealousy.

To Gerard's pleasure, Britt did as he encouraged. He

turned his back on Rawlins while kicking his legs and heading toward the surface. Gerard followed suit, swishing his tail, even as he began to shift.

Back in human form, Gerard broke the surface. He took a deep breath as he shoved his hair away from his face. Peering around, he spotted Britt treading water while pushing the mask on top of his head.

Gerard spotted Rawlins swimming toward the beach and hollered, "Thanks, man." Grinning, he added, "It's always so much fun to swim with ya."

Rawlins peered over his shoulder at him, smirking. "You're welcome." He jerked his chin in Britt's direction. "Who's your friend?"

Somehow, Gerard's grin managed to widen. "This is Britt O'Connor. He's my mate," he stated proudly. "Met him this mornin'."

"Really?" Rawlins paused and turned to face them. His attention moved to Britt. "And you're swimming together already? Already had an interest in paranormal stuff, Britt?"

"No." Britt sported a rueful expression. "But I worked with Price in the military and already knew he was something . . . *other*." He shrugged his wide shoulders, making the water ripple around him. "Guess if vampires are real, shifters isn't much of a leap."

Rawlins chuckled. "Guess not." He began swimming backward toward the shore once more. "Well, congratulations." With a waggle of his eyebrows, Rawlins started to turn away as he added, "Finding your mate is a real cause for joy. Have a fun night."

"Thanks, Rawlins. I sure hope to." Gerard bit back a laugh because he spotted the slight darkening of Britt's cheeks and scented a hint of embarrassment from the man. Knowing Rawlins was about to exit the water, Gerard cleared his throat.

"Uh, can I get ya to focus on me or turn around, please?" Seeing Britt arch one brow in obvious question, he explained, "Rawlins is about to get out of the pool, and he's naked, ya know. He'll grab a towel and get outta here." Gerard knew from the way the water was splashing that Rawlins was doing exactly as he said. "Then we can head up, too."

Britt nodded once as he turned to put his back mostly toward the stairs. "So, uh . . . what exactly is Rawlins?"

CHAPTER SIX

"An ammonite." Britt repeated Gerard's answer. Racking his brain, he slowly shook his head. "Never heard of it."

Gerard glanced over his shoulder, then began swimming toward shore. "Come on," he encouraged, doing a slow breaststroke. "And that's because they're extinct in the wild. Rawlins can swim around here because of some technological scrambler thingy that Ovram installed over the coastal waters. It stops radar and shit from spotting us." With a wink, Gerard added, "Maybe ask him about it. You'd probably understand that shit. I'm just grateful it works."

Britt nodded slowly, making a mental note to do that. Whatever the device was, it sounded fascinating. He wondered why the military or some government agency never came knocking on these guys' door about the interference. Britt didn't bother asking, though, knowing from Gerard's words that he wouldn't know the answer.

As soon as Britt reached where he could touch, the flippers slowed his movements. He decided to swim as close as possible. Once he was nearly crawling, he turned and planted his butt in the surf so he could remove them.

With the flippers in hand, Britt rose to his feet and turned, intending to finish leaving the water. Instead, he froze. His attention fell on Gerard, who was leaning over and picking up his shirt. Britt nearly swallowed his tongue as he took in Gerard's naked ass. The gorgeous muscles flexed enticingly as Gerard straightened.

Britt tried to swallow his moan as his blood flashed hot

within him. His arousal surged, and his mouth watered for a taste of that. Even the discomfort of his dick filling behind a neoprene suit didn't lessen his sudden need.

Then Gerard turned, and Britt enjoyed the view all over again. The shifter's prick was longer than what he would have guessed for a man his size—probably nine inches. With his toned abdominals and sensual vee, his body seemed to be pointing straight at that prize.

While it had been more years than Britt could recall since he'd sucked cock, he suddenly felt the need to drop to his knees and worship that thing of beauty.

"I like the way you're lookin' at me, Britt," Gerard stated, his voice deep and sultry. "There's no sense in denyin' our needs."

Hearing those words, Britt snapped his attention to Gerard's face. His breath caught for a new reason. The lust blazing in the shifter's blue eyes spoke of all kinds of carnal delights.

Britt's breath caught in his chest, and his prick thickened to full mast. His head actually felt lightheaded from the sudden blood loss. The desire to strip and sample everything Gerard was offering hit him like a one-two punch to the gut.

"Mind if I come over there and strip that suit off ya, Britt?"

Gerard rumbled the words as he began stalking forward slowly. He was obviously giving him time to respond. That didn't make it any easier for Britt to find his tongue.

Hell, with each step, Gerard's erection twitched at his groin. Britt couldn't stop staring. He licked his lips as he watched the man's foreskin pull back, revealing his red, swollen head.

"I need ya to talk to me, my mate," Gerard crooned, stopping before him. He settled his hand on Britt's neck just above the collar of his wetsuit. "I need words."

Hearing the word mate, Britt finally yanked his attention

up to Gerard's face. "Mate," he muttered. When he saw the shifter's eyes light up, he knew the man had misunderstood. Resting his palm on Gerard's chest, Britt quickly amended, "If we fuck, you're going to think I'm accepting this mate-thing. Aren't you?"

Britt watched Gerard's jaw clench, and a muscle ticked there just a little. The move betrayed his disappointment, and for some reason, Britt suddenly felt like a heel. Even though Britt didn't understand why he needed that expression cleared up, he followed his instincts.

"Try not to take offense, Gerard," Britt murmured softly. Dipping his head the couple of inches of height difference, he bussed his lips over the other man's. "I don't" — seeing Gerard narrow his eyes just a little more, he quickly amended — "I'm not built like you, like a shifter. I've never jumped into anything with both feet before. I need . . . time still, to wrap my head around this."

As Britt talked, he watched the tightness from Gerard's features ease. To his surprise, seeing that caused his own excitement to rise. Britt had always been a little bit of a control freak. Even the military hadn't beaten that out of him, so he liked being able to affect Gerard in such a way.

When has pleasing someone else brought me such gratification?

That knowledge caused him to tense a smidge.

"Yeah, I'll want to bond us, Britt," Gerard admitted softly while offering a reassuring smile. "But it doesn't have to be today." Swiping his tongue over his lower lip, Gerard offered, "Why dontcha kiss me proper? Like I said before, there's no sense in denyin' our needs." His voice turned husky. "We'll leave the question of bonding to another day. How's that sound?"

Relief filled Britt, and he expected that. What he hadn't expected was to also feel a measure of disappointment. Britt just didn't know why, so he pushed it from his mind.

49

I'm not ready to commit to this whole shifter mates thing anyway.

After thinking that, Britt shut down any more stray ideas and did as Gerard had advised. He cradled the man's smooth jaw in one hand while wrapping his other arm around his waist. Dipping his head, Britt took his first true taste of the man's distracting mouth. Immediately, Gerard opened to him, and Britt took complete advantage, sliding his tongue in deep.

Britt felt Gerard press against him and mentally cursed the wetsuit he still wore. Then his mind shut down with the deep masculine flavor of the man who was about to become his lover. The heady flavors exploded across his tongue, and he fed the other man a growl as he tightened the arm around his waist.

Sliding his hand down, Britt gripped one of Gerard's firm cheeks and squeezed. He moaned again, relishing the hard muscle he held. Needing more, Britt snapped his head up, breaking the kiss.

"I need to fuck you," Britt declared. Then, recalling where they were, he growled in annoyance. "Where can we go?"

Gerard barely wanted to go five feet, let alone climb half a dozen stairs. Fortunately, he knew they wouldn't need to. He flexed his ass cheek, pleased to feel Britt's fingers twitch where he gripped him.

"We don't need to go anywhere," Gerard told him as he reached behind Britt and gripped the strap attached to the zipper. He began pulling it down, exposing his sexy human as he used his chin to indicate toward the left. "See that rock there?"

"Yeah," Britt replied, his voice deep from his arousal. Looking confused, he quickly added, "Why are we discussing a rock?" His brows furrowed. "And unless you have lube in those shorts in the sand, we're definitely going to have to go somewhere."

Finishing unzipping his mate's wetsuit, Gerard told him, "Well, that ain't really a rock."

Gerard slid his hand into the open back and teased his fingertips along the top of Britt's crack. He liked the sound of Britt's quickly indrawn breath. Using a fingernail, he scraped the sensitive skin lightly, earning a very pleasant-sounding hiss.

"Then what is it?" Britt growled, his green eyes dark with arousal. Then he tensed. "Or are you stalling? You don't bottom?"

"I'll bottom for ya," Gerard replied in lieu of a true answer. Seeing Britt's disbelieving expression, he smiled and admitted, "I'm a switch, Britt. And I'll take ya any way I can get ya."

Never have I spoken truer words.

Gerard wanted his mate, desperately.

"Then what's the hold-up in going somewhere?" Britt asked gruffly. His fingers twitched on Gerard's ass again. The tips of them even sank in between his cheeks to tease his crease.

Groaning, Gerard arched his back and pressed into his mate's touch. "I mean," he muttered, starting to pant. "I mean, that ain't a rock. It's a storage closet."

Since Gerard knew Britt was focused on him when Rawlins had exited the water, he figured his human hadn't even noticed.

"And you have lube in there?" Britt's voice came out gruff, and he tensed in Gerard's hold. "You bring tricks down here often?"

While Gerard silently reveled in Britt's show of jealousy, he didn't draw attention to it. Instead, he told him, "No, I've never brought a trick here. None of us have." Seeing Britt's disbelieving expression, Gerard explained, "Our alpha has few hard and fast rules, but never bringin' anyone but members of the pod here is one of them. No one would ever break it."

"But I'm not a member of the pod," Britt pointed out, scowling at him. "So—"

Moving a hand up, Gerard pressed his fingertips to his lips, silencing him. "But ya are my mate." He traced his fingers along the scar that ran from the edge of his jaw up to behind his ear, wondering how his mate had gotten it. "I know ya don't want to hear it, yet, but that means you're part of the pod, bonded or not." Gerard used a thumb to gently massage the edge of his mate's furrowed brow. "That means ya can be here."

Britt must have decided to move past the whole mate discussion—again—for instead, he asked, "Then why the lube in the closet?"

"Because there are plenty of people in my pod who've found their mates, so they come here for picnics and to swim." Waggling his brows, Gerard told him, "Paranormals have a hard time keepin' their hands off their partners, and when they're wet and half naked?" He snorted as he glanced meaningfully at the water. "This beach has seen a helluva lot of action, so lube's kept here now."

"Aren't you worried someone will walk"—Britt glanced toward the water—"or swim in on us?"

Recalling Britt mentioning he wasn't into exhibitionism, Gerard assured, "Even if someone came upon us, they'd turn around right quick."

"Why?" Britt obviously didn't believe him.

"I know ya don't understand, but the bond between mates is sacred," Gerard tried to explain. "They wouldn't intrude unless it was a matter of life and death."

Britt held his gaze for a long moment, staring into his eyes. "Okay," he said finally, releasing his hold and backing up a step. "Grab the lube." His smile turned lopsided. "And a couple of towels. I don't fancy sand in certain places. It'd remind me too much of Afghanistan."

"You got it."

Gerard hurried to the storage closet disguised as a boulder. Feeling around the left edge, he found the hidden latch and opened it. He snagged what he needed quickly enough before closing the door once more.

When Gerard turned back toward Britt, it took every last bit of self-control he had not to stand there and drool. He swallowed convulsively as he strode across the sand. His cock throbbed as he took in the specimen of masculinity before him.

While Gerard had known that Britt was a soldier, a Navy SEAL, his hard body told the tale. Scars decorated his flesh in various locations, and Gerard wanted the chance to hear the story of each . . . right after he'd kissed and licked them. Although Britt's stomach didn't sport a six-pack, his abdominals were flat and strong, the flesh of his body toned.

"Now who looks like they want to eat someone," Britt stated, smirking. He lowered his hand to grip the hard shaft jutting from his groin and gave himself a couple of leisurely strokes. "I want this in your ass as swiftly as possible, Gerard," he demanded. "Don't make me wait."

A shiver of anticipation ran up Gerard's spine upon hearing the command in Britt's voice. "Anythin' ya want, my mate," he murmured, unable to help himself.

Britt growled softly as he held out his second hand. "Give me the lube." Once Gerard did it, he told him, "Lay out the towel, then get on it in the middle on your hands and knees, ass toward me."

Gerard's erection jerked with anticipation as he followed his mate's instruction. He'd grabbed two towels, so he spread them both, offering them more room. Easing to his knees,

Gerard peered over his shoulder just in time to see Britt greasing his pole.

"Hands and knees," Britt ordered again, his voice gruff and low.

Immediately obeying, Gerard rested his weight on his hands. Then he lowered to his forearms and arched his back in invitation. Hearing Britt's low growl, the sound one of pleasure, Gerard felt as if his heart skipped a beat.

Hell, yeah. I'm pleasing my mate. Finally.

A second later, Gerard felt the towels shift behind him. Then Britt's large, calloused hand landed on his ass cheek. His big human didn't ask permission. He just used the hold to spread him a little before drizzling lube onto his crack.

Goose bumps broke out on Gerard's thighs upon feeling the chilly liquid, even as his cock jerked and throbbed. Feeling Britt's fingers massage the slick into his opening, he moaned with pleasure. The hairs on his nape stood on end, and he couldn't help rocking back into Britt's touch.

"So eager," Britt rumbled, popping a finger inside him. "God, it's a good look on you." He fingered him deeply for a few seconds. "Can't wait to feel this wrapped around my cock."

"Yessss," Gerard hissed, pushing into Britt's ministrations. Having never been a passive lover, he demanded, "Another. I want it."

"You'll get it and more," Britt replied, giving him a second finger.

The stretch of his mate's fingers in him caused tingles of pleasure to burst through Gerard, scorching his nerve endings in the best of ways. He feared he would go off like a rocket at any second. When Britt added a third finger and rubbed over his prostate, Gerard moaned loudly.

"That's right. Tell me how good it feels."

Twisting his fingers into the towel, Gerard groaned again. "Britt," he whined, need riding him hard. "Please don't make me wait. Need you."

"Got me," Britt replied, his voice deep and gruff. "Here I come."

Gerard felt his heart soar upon those simple words, even as he tried to remind himself that Britt was just stating them in the heat of the moment. Then he felt the touch of Britt's thick crown at his opening, and all thoughts fled. As soon as Gerard felt Britt pressing against him, he pushed out and rocked back at the same time.

Britt's big tool burrowed deep inside Gerard's body, stretching him and filling him in the most intimate and perfect of ways. Growling, Britt didn't stop pushing until he was seated fully inside him. Gerard loved every inch of it.

Absolutely perfect.

"Fuck," Britt snarled, planting his left hand on the towel beside Gerard's. He snaked his right arm around Gerard's waist, holding him tightly in place. "Stay still."

Gerard groaned as he was held in place. "Britt," he whined, shuddering beneath the larger man. "Please."

"I said stay still," Britt demanded again before nipping at Gerard's neck. "I'm close to losin' it."

With a grin, Gerard tightened his chute muscles once, twice, and on the third time, he heard Britt's low rumbling growl before his mate snapped, "You asked for it."

Britt pulled most of the way out before snapping his hips forward again. He did it over and over, driving deeply into Gerard's body with single-minded abandon. Every few strokes, Britt nailed Gerard's prostate, winding him higher and higher.

With a mighty roar, Britt slammed home once more, and Gerard felt his human's hot cum flood his body, marking him internally. His own bliss rose to meet it, and his orgasm crashed over him. Unloading pulse after pulse of seed into the towel beneath him, Gerard rode the best release of his life, knowing he'd pleased his mate.

Chapter Seven

Britt floated languidly, his senses blissed-out from the best release he could ever remember. With his bare prick encased in Gerard's gripping body, he couldn't find it in himself to pull out. Instead, Britt used the last of his dwindling energy to encourage his lover to ease onto his side.

Spooning behind Gerard, Britt kept him wrapped in his arms. He absently petted the shifter's abdominals, tracing along the grooves of his six-pack, then down the line of his vee. Reaching Gerard's prick, Britt found it half-hard and couldn't resist wrapping his fingers around it. He rubbed his thumb along the crown, playing with the foreskin a little, finding it still damp from his release.

Gerard groaned softly and trembled against him.

Chuckling softly, Britt kissed the back of Gerard's neck, then released his lover's dick. The shifter groaned for a new reason. He even peered over his shoulder and scowled at him.

"Tease," Gerard grumbled.

Surprised, Britt arched a brow. "I was worried you were too sensitive," he admitted. "That I was hurting you."

Gerard shrugged one shoulder. "Sorta hurt, but still felt good." Relaxing back against him, he murmured, "Was making me hard again."

"Really?" Britt was having a hard time believing that. "You could really get it up again?"

At fifty-four, Britt was damn certain his days of back-to-back orgasms were over. Still, if he could give that to Gerard, he would enjoy seeing it. They weren't keeping score, after all.

"Yeah." Gerard cleared his throat, then revealed, "A shifter's sex drive is naturally higher than a human's, but once we meet our mate, it escalates even more." Squeezing his chute muscles, he massaged Britt's still-embedded cock. "I could get you up again, too."

When Gerard did it again, Britt groaned softly, enjoying the exquisite sensations. "Damn," he muttered, pressing his forehead into Gerard's shoulder. "I just thought I was still half-hard because I didn't pull out. Never gone without a rubber before," he admitted. "Wanted to enjoy the feeling as long as I could."

Britt didn't say it, but he wanted to remember the feeling long after he was gone. Except, that was when it occurred to him. For the first time in all his years of having sex, he didn't feel a driving need to get away from his partner of the moment. Instead, Britt wanted to stay right there and enjoy another round.

Can't say as I've ever felt that way before.

When Britt felt Gerard squeeze him once more, then begin to roll his hips a little, causing him to slide out and back in just a smidge, Britt gave up thinking about it.

I'll worry about it later.

Britt returned his hand to Gerard's prick, surprised to find it was indeed hard again. Going with it, he began jacking the other man's considerable length. He recalled what it looked like, and he was damn tempted to roll the man to his back so he could suck it.

Except, that would mean pulling out, and Britt couldn't bear to lose the exquisite heat wrapped around his dick.

"Damn," Britt mumbled, rutting slowly. He felt heat quickly fill his groin as his balls once more began to tingle. "Never felt anything like this."

With a soft growl, Gerard rumbled, "And ya never will again." He clamped down extra-hard on Britt's erection the next time he was buried deep.

Britt froze and groaned, a shudder working through him as he nearly lost it just from that. Unable to help himself, he began speeding up. His balls felt heavy and full, and he didn't know how it was possible, but the tingle at the base of his spine told him he didn't have long.

Wanting Gerard right there with him, Britt began working the man's cock in earnest. He teased under the foreskin on each upstroke, smearing the pre-cum leaking from his slit. He massaged his frenulum, working the bundle of sensitive nerves. Gripping the base of his lover's shaft, Britt squeezed tighter on the next upstroke. On the downstroke, he paused to cradle Gerard's balls, rolling them lightly.

"Oh, fuck," Gerard cried, a whine in his voice.

Growling in Gerard's ear, Britt did it again, realizing he'd found a hot spot. His shifter liked his balls played with. He couldn't wait to drag those sorts of noises out of the man when he suckled on them.

Before Britt could freak out at his thoughts, another one of Gerard's squeezes to his shaft sent him tumbling over the edge. He roared with ecstasy as he poured shot after shot into Gerard's willing chute. On instinct, at the same time, Britt squeezed his lover's balls.

Gerard let out a loud groan as his body jolted. That was followed by a second shudder. Then he moaned as he sagged back against Britt, his breathing noisy as he relaxed on the towels.

With a sigh, Britt released Gerard's balls. He moved his hand back to his shifter's abdominals. As much as Britt wanted to just bask in the afterglow, his mind began to whirl, and he couldn't seem to stop it.

Trepidation and confusion filled Britt in equal measure. His life was already being turned upside-down by the people hunting him. How could he accept this, too?

Besides, what would happen when Gerard's friends figured out who was after him? Britt knew he would need to
leave to take care of the problem. He couldn't continue to put
these people at risk.

Except, for the first time in his life, Britt didn't want to
move after sex. He didn't want to release the handsome man
in his arms. He didn't want to contemplate not being able to
do this again . . . and more.

Something must have tipped off Gerard to Britt's freak-out,
for he murmured, "You're thinkin' awfully hard back there."
He moved his hand to Gerard's wrist and squeezed lightly.
"Do ya wanna talk about it? Maybe I can help."

To Britt's surprise, he opened his mouth without conscious
thought and shared, "I don't want to leave."

Gerard chuckled softly. "Me, either." His voice filled with
warmth. "Your hands are golden, mate. And your dick feels
fantastic stretchin' me." Then Gerard wriggled a little, his
head moving. "Although, I wouldn't mind doin' this in a bed
next time."

"You misunderstand me." Britt knew he had to set the
shifter straight. "I've never wanted to lie with a lover before.
I don't cuddle. I don't even want to stay in the same bed. I
leave." Britt felt tension in the body of the man before him,
and he couldn't seem to shut his mouth. "But with you . . .
with you, I'm happy to just lie here and . . . bask. I've never
done that before." With a scoff, Britt added, "And I've certainly not started to think about what I want to do to you next
round. This isn't how I act." Confused as hell, Britt muttered,
"Why do I feel like this now? Why you?"

Issuing a deep, quiet sigh, Gerard turned his head a little
and peered at him over his shoulder. "I don't mean to beat a
dead horse, but I'm a shifter, and you're my mate." He
shrugged his shoulders, and a wry smile curved his lips. "It
really is as simple as that. You're the other half of my soul,

just like I'm the other half of yours. We're meant to be together."

Instead of trying to refute that again—*hell, I may be a stubborn cuss, but I'm not an idiot*—because Britt could see the connection, could feel it, he asked, "What happens when I need to leave to take care of the people after me? What—"

"Then I go with ya," Gerard declared, cutting him off. Unexpectedly, the shifter moved. He rocked forward, pulling free of Britt's softened prick. Rolling and utilizing impressive strength, Gerard pushed Britt to his back. He leaned over him and held his gaze with a serious look in his blue eyes. "I get you're a loner, Britt, but if you're goin' somewhere dangerous, then I'll be right there at your side. Get me? You're my mate."

As Britt stared up at Gerard, something odd and warm settled in his gut.

Huh. Maybe it really is just that simple.

Gerard waited with bated breath for Britt's response. He didn't know if blunt was the way to go with his human. He didn't know him well enough, yet. In this case, however, Gerard couldn't help but put his foot down.

No way is my mate goin' off to fight some assholes and leavin' me behind.

It just wasn't happening. Gerard would tie Britt to the bed first, shifter instincts to please his mate be damned.

Mmmm . . . my mate tied to a bed . . .

Squashing that line of thought before it distracted him too much, he refocused on Britt. To Gerard's surprise, he watched the corners of the soldier's hard mouth twitch. Then Britt scoffed softly, as if a thought had just occurred to him.

"I guess . . . it really is just that simple with you guys, isn't it?"

Gerard wasn't entirely certain what Britt was asking, so he

decided to take it at face value. "Yeah," he confirmed. "It's that simple. If I know you're goin' somewhere dangerous, I go with ya."

"Because I'm your mate."

Dipping his chin in a firm nod, Gerard replied, "Yeah."

"Even though we're not bonded yet."

Gerard's breath caught in his chest. He wasn't certain what to make of that *yet* part. "Yeah," he responded again. Deciding to push it just a little, he added, "Besides, once we bond, we're not gonna wanna be apart for too long of periods, anyway." With a shrug, Gerard raked his gaze over Britt's handsome frame heatedly. "Alpha Kaiser normally gives shifters at least a week off after bondin', to give them time to settle in together." Growling softly, Gerard felt his arousal surge anew as he enjoyed the view of his human sprawled under him. "It gives us time to get our ragin' libidos under control so we can stand bein' away from each other for a few hours a day."

Britt lifted his hands and placed them on Gerard's shoulders. His eyes narrowed as he began gently massaging him. He worked one arm around Gerard's back and began rubbing along the knobs of his spine. Britt moved his other hand to Gerard's front and began exploring his pectorals.

Desire roaring through him once more, Gerard growled softly as a tremble worked through him. "What ya doin', mate?" he growled when Britt tweaked his nipple.

"Figured I'd rev you up a little, so we can get to that bonding thing, hmm?"

Gerard groaned, and as much as he wanted that, too, he gritted his teeth. He forced himself to take a noisy breath in through his nose. Then he scowled at Britt and warned, "This ain't somethin' to joke about, Britt."

Britt's smile appeared fond, and he glided the hand up Gerard's back to cradle his nape. "Not joking, shifter," he told him in a serious tone. "Although I understand why you'd get that idea." His dark brows creased as he glanced away for a second. When Britt met his gaze again, he told him, "I'm old, and it sometimes takes me a bit to wrap my brain around new things, but I'm not stupid. I wouldn't let something as simple and straightforward as this, something that could turn wonderful, get away." With a wry smile, Britt stated, "I suppose I could put my failsafe in place. As much as I love my mountain home, I bet there's plenty of other places you can show me around here. I've always enjoyed scuba diving."

Realization hit.

"Gods, you're serious."

Nodding, Britt replied, "As a heart attack."

"Once we bond, I don't think you'll have to worry about those." Gerard stiffened as he gasped. "Damn. Have ya had one of those before?"

"Fortunately, no," Britt replied with a chuckle. "I've always had pretty good health."

"Good." Excitement of a different sort coursed through Gerard. "And now your health will get even better."

Britt nodded. "I remember Price rattling off the perks," he admitted. "Better senses, heightened strength, stronger bones, greater resistance to illness."

"Is that why you're agreein'?" Gerard couldn't help but ask.

Would it really matter if it was? I still get my mate.

"No," Britt instantly replied. "How I respond to you . . . I've never felt it before. It's . . . disconcerting." Shrugging one shoulder, Britt smiled at him. "But I like it."

Although Gerard hated to admit it, relief flooded him.

Guess it did matter to me, but I would have taken my mate any way I could get him and somehow convinced him that he'd made the best choice. Now, I don't have to worry about that . . . although I'll still prove this is the best choice.

"Now then." Britt glanced around for a few seconds before grabbing something. When he held it up, Gerard saw the tube of lube. "I haven't bottomed in a really long time, but I'd still like to do this on my back. I'd like to see you."

Gerard took the lube with a nod. He realized it had to be the whole control thing. That was okay. They had centuries to learn each other's quirks.

"Anythin' ya want, mate," Gerard crooned as he eased between Britt's legs. Noticing the tension in the limbs, he knew just how to ease it. "Let's get ya cleaned up a smidge."

Reaching over, Gerard grabbed one of the bottles of water he'd brought from the supply cupboard, too. He quickly went about cleaning Britt's groin, using a corner of one of the towels. As Gerard dried him, he was a little surprised Britt allowed the intimate act, even though he watched him like a hawk.

"Why?" Britt finally asked.

Resting on his knees, Gerard set the nearly empty bottle of water aside and picked up the lube. He met Britt's gaze and grinned.

"Because I'm gonna suck your dick as I open ya."

Before Britt could respond, Gerard did exactly that, driving his mate out of his mind with distraction.

Chapter Eight

Just as Gerard had predicted, Alpha Kaiser had given the shifter the week off.

Britt couldn't remember the last time he'd spent so much time in someone's company. It had to have been when he was back in the service. After all, orders were orders.

Walking toward Ovram's office, Britt thought he should be relieved that after a week in Gerard's company, his lover was back at work. The old him would definitely have been ready for some space. Hell, he would have run after the first fuck in the grotto.

Not now, though.

Instead, Britt realized he actually missed Gerard . . . and the man had only been gone two hours. He'd learned that his lover was the announcer for *World of Aquatica's* extremely popular tiger shark show. Nowhere in the world was there a show showcasing a tiger shark.

Even though Britt had learned that the three tiger sharks who acted in the show were shifters, he was still damn impressed. After all, they had to learn cues just like other performers. On top of that, the tiger sharks had to act a certain way in order to always fool the humans.

Yep. Damn impressive.

Reaching the door to Ovram's office at the main complex — the sea lion shifter had an office at the park as well as an even larger one in the main headquarters of the shifter community — something he called his command center. That was where Ovram had asked to meet him. The shifter wanted to review the information he'd gathered.

After Britt knocked twice, he heard Ovram's shouted, "Enter."

Britt opened the door and headed inside. Unable to help himself, he whistled low under his breath. In the past, Ovram had stopped by Gerard's suite with his laptop or tablet. This was the first time Britt had seen Ovram's office, and to say he was impressed was an understatement.

Command center is right.

The space was the size of a small conference room. Ovram certainly knew his toys. There was a wall of monitors, four keyboards in front of the man, and banks of hard drives. The room was even chilled enough that Britt wished he'd worn long sleeves.

Ovram chuckled as he spun in his chair, taking in his expression. "Yeah, we take our safety very seriously here, Britt." Then he beckoned to a rolling stool pushed under a counter. "Grab that and come here. I have info on our friend."

Doing as he was told, Britt grabbed the stool and moved it to Ovram's side. As he sat, he noticed the stranger's face on one of the monitors. Another monitor contained a dossier on the guy. Reading the first few lines, recognition hit Britt.

"Well, shit," Britt whispered, shaking his head.

"So, you recognize him now?" Ovram smirked at him.

Britt nodded. "Javier Lopez is the younger brother of a guy who used to work as an enforcer for a cartel I helped take down. They were running the usual, but they were also in the slave market for young girls." Curling his lip, he recalled the group. "I provided the information to a black ops group through an anonymous handle, and they took damn near the entire organization down." Pointing at the picture of the dark-haired Hispanic man, Britt told him, "Javier's older brother died in the raid. Javier wasn't much more than a foot soldier last year."

"A little more than a foot soldier," Ovram corrected, putting more information on another screen. "Evidently, he and his brother hid it well, but they were angling to take out leadership and take over the business." Shaking his head, Ovram sneered with disgust. "When his brother was killed, Javier went underground, but he still had connections and money." Ovram pointed at the screen. "He's the one who paid a hacker to track you down."

When Ovram put another picture on the screen, Britt winced as he took in the dark-haired male's features. "The guy's just a kid."

Ovram nodded. "Nineteen, but yeah." Sadness crossed his face as he met Britt's gaze. "From what I understand, it's blackmail. He does this, or his sister gets sold. They're reforming the slave ring."

"The hell they are," Britt declared, already mentally flipping through who to contact about it.

"Relax, Britt," Alpha Kaiser stated, striding into the room. "We won't let that happen." While he smiled, it didn't reach his intense green eyes. "But we'll discuss that at another time." Crossing his arms over his chest, Kaiser frowned at him. "Why do I have your boss, Lucas, at my gates insisting on speaking with you?"

"Uhhhh." After that really eloquent response, Britt snapped his mouth shut and shook his head. "I don't know."

Recalling his interrupted call a week earlier, Britt told the shifter leader about it.

"Well, let's go see how big of a problem Lucas is going to be," Alpha Kaiser stated, beckoning toward the still-open door. As Britt began moving through it, Kaiser ordered, "Ovram, let me know immediately if you find anything at all regarding Javier's location."

"On it, Alpha," Ovram replied. "It'll only be a matter of time."

Alpha Kaiser took Britt to a meeting room on the first floor. As opposed to the lounge, this room boasted a large desk and décor that screamed alpha male—*I'm in charge.* There were two sofas—one arranged to the left of the desk while the other was on the wall next to the door. Two chairs faced the desk.

"Take that sofa, Britt," Alpha Kaiser ordered, pointing to the one to the left of the desk. The alpha hit a button on the desk and ordered, "Show him in."

Eban entered with Lucas.

Britt immediately noticed the tell-tale bulge under his boss's suit jacket. He was armed.

Lucas glanced over his shoulder, obviously noticing Eban positioning himself near the second sofa by the door. Shaking his head, his boss focused on Britt.

"I need you to come with me, Britt," Lucas ordered with an imperious wave of his hand. "You should have notified me immediately about your problem instead of involving outsiders. People coming after one of ours should have been kept in-house." With a cold smile, Lucas added, "After all, we certainly don't want it getting out that we can't keep one of our own safe. Who would hire us then?"

"Exactly why I didn't mention it," Britt countered, not moving an inch. "This is personal business, and I didn't want the company implicated."

Or involved.

"Well, you're not going to get what you want." Lucas pulled the gun from his jacket and pointed it at Alpha Kaiser. "Come with me now, or this office is going to get very messy."

Alpha Kaiser looked bored as he stated drolly, "Better aim for the head. Either way, you shoot and you'll be dead in two seconds."

Scoffing, Lucas sneered as he cut a glance toward Eban. Evidently, he decided to rethink his position, for he held up his phone. There was a video playing on it.

"Maybe you'll do it for your little boy-toy then." Lucas

chuckled coldly. "A cute blond like him? Javier will have no trouble selling his ass."

Britt growled low in his throat, anger surging through him. "You're involved with their trafficking ring?" He'd always thought Lucas was a bit of an ass, but he never would have seen that coming.

"Naw," Lucas admitted. "Course not, but you're worth a lot of money to Javier, Britt." Chuckling, the sound one of cruelty, he stated, "You stuck your nose in where it doesn't belong. If I don't walk out of here with you and call to confirm in five minutes, Javier's going to kidnap your boy-toy. I'm sure he'll show him how a real man does it before selling his ass." Lowering his voice to a sinister hiss, Lucas finished, "I hear Javier likes that kind of shit."

"Let's do this instead," Price rumbled, arriving through a concealed entrance to the left. His eyes glowed red. "Let's have you tell Javier that you have him, so he thinks everything is fine."

A second later, Lucas's expression sagged. He lowered the gun, and his face grew slack.

Damn. Vampires have some freaky skills. Glad he's on our side. Still —

Britt rushed from the room, needing to get to Gerard.

"Those cement stairs are wet, ladies and gentlemen, so remember to walk, be careful, and take your time," Gerard stated through his microphone as he heard and saw people start preparing to leave. "And thank you so much for visitin' *World of Aquatica*. Have a great rest of your day."

As much as Gerard loved his job, he missed his mate. He'd always known the first day back would be the hardest. Leaving his sexy human drinking a cup of coffee and reading something on a borrowed laptop had been the most difficult thing he'd ever done in his life.

Still, Gerard knew it had to be done. He couldn't live in Britt's pocket all the time. They had separate lives, after all.

At least Britt won't be going anywhere after this.

Gerard had been there when Alpha Kaiser had stopped by his apartment. The alpha had offered Britt a position on their electronics team. Essentially, Britt would work with Ovram in research and keeping their place safe.

Britt had accepted.

That evening, Gerard had watched Britt institute the fail-safe he'd mentioned. In essence, he'd blown up the propane tank on his property. The findings would be that the valve had been faulty, had created a spark, and Britt's home had gone up in spectacular display . . . according to a hidden camera on Britt's property. His human intended to continue to monitor the area for problems.

He's mine. He's staying with me.

Gerard couldn't believe how settled that had made not only him but his sea dragon feel.

"Excuse me, sir."

The young woman's voice drew Gerard's attention back to where it should be — work. As he turned to face her, he hoped she wasn't going to try hitting on him. While Gerard figured he would still find it flattering, he always hated dashing people's hopes.

Maybe I should wear a wedding ring. That way it won't be a surprise when I say no.

Fortunately, instead of hitting on him, the woman held up a map of the park. "Can you show me the safest route to the underground aquarium?" Waving a hand, she indicated a man in a wheelchair waiting a few paces away. "Something easy for my husband to navigate?"

"Of course." Gerard pointed at the map, indicating the needed route. "This here'll get ya to the elevator. Did ya get the code from the office?"

"Yes, sir. We got it when we picked up our reservations."

The woman smiled up at him gratefully. "Thanks so much." She moved closer to her husband and, while waving, added, "The show was amazing!"

With a wave and a smile, Gerard replied, "I'm glad ya enjoyed it."

Gerard turned his attention to watching the exiting crowd once more. There were only a few people left taking pictures of the tiger shark. In this case, it was River who'd performed the show.

Just as the last few stragglers started toward the door, Gerard felt the hairs on his neck stand on end. He began to turn, trying to locate the source of his unease, but a hand grabbed his upper arm. The feel of a gun barrel pressed into his side caused him to freeze for a few seconds.

That was long enough for the others to file out of the stadium, leaving him alone with the man.

"You're comin' with me, pretty boy," the man stated, his voice colored by a slight Spanish accent. "Your fag boyfriend cost me someone, and now he's gonna pay." He chuckled sinisterly as he added, "Or you and me are gonna get real friendly."

With the way the guy bumped his groin against Gerard's side, there was no doubt about what he meant.

Not a chance.

"Where are we goin'?" Gerard asked, looking over his shoulder at the guy. To his surprise, he recognized the dark-haired, Hispanic man—sort of. "It's you." He couldn't help blurting out the words. "You attacked Britt at his house."

This man had been the team leader of the mercenaries.

"Yeah, I did," the man declared. "I wanna know how the fuck he escaped."

"Because he's smarter than ya," Gerard goaded. "He ain't no dumb shmuck criminal."

"I'm no dumb shmuck!" the man screamed.

At the same time, he lifted the gun and attempted to pistol

whip him.

Gerard took the opportunity. He wrapped both arms around his attacker and lunged toward the pool. With his shifter strength, Gerard easily propelled them both into the water.

Instead of surfacing, Gerard sank . . . and shifted. As a smaller shifter, he knew he could figure out a way out of his clothes. Just as he completed his change and found himself tangled in his polo shirt, Gerard heard the unmistakable sound of a gun, even under the water.

He wriggled this way and that, trying to get out.

Just as Gerard managed to slip free of the polo shirt, he heard a scream. The scent of blood bloomed in the water. Gerard looked frantically around, searching.

Then Gerard relaxed and shook his head, relief flooding him.

River had bitten the gunman's arm clean off. Currently, the man was flailing and screaming as he bled in the water. The human kept trying to get away from River, who circled and feinted attacks at him.

"Gerard? You in there?" Alpha Kaiser's face appeared above, marred by the water.

Next to him, Britt held out his hand. "Come on, lover," his human urged, wiggling his fingers. "Let's get out of here."

A second later, Eban and Dare dove into the water and began swimming toward the gunman.

Gerard shifted.

Back in human form, Gerard reached up and grabbed his mate's hand. Britt hauled him out of the water. Alpha Kaiser held out his coat, and Gerard wrapped it around his waist. A second later, Britt yanked him close, enfolding him in his arms. Returning the embrace, Gerard was only too happy to stay snuggled close against his taciturn human as he watched

Eban and Dare drag an unconscious — or maybe dead — gunman from the pool.

Doc Anthony cleared it up a few seconds later when he announced, "He's dead, Alpha."

Alpha Kaiser nodded. "For the best."

"Who was he?" Gerard asked.

After Britt explained who Javier was and why he'd not only wanted Britt dead but why he'd come after him, Gerard had to agree.

Good riddance to bad rubbish.

River's head appeared over the side of the pool, having changed to human form. "You owe me a fucking bottle of tequila, Gerard," he declared with a grimace. "I hate the taste of human, and he was extra nasty."

Laughing, Gerard nodded. "I owe ya more than a bottle, my friend. I'll make it a case."

Taking the toothbrush and toothpaste provided by the doc, River gave him a *thumbs up* as he brushed.

"We'll have to drain the aquarium and sanitize it." Alpha Kaiser shook his head, looking disgusted as he eyed the red-tinged water. "Good thing it was already the second show of the day." Then the alpha followed Eban, Dare, and Doc Anthony as they used the back tunnels to move Javier's body. "Have a good night, gentlemen. Enjoy winner's sex."

"Winner's sex?" Britt muttered, frowning. "What's he mean?"

Gerard chuckled low in his throat as he pressed his body tighter to his mate's. "To the victor go the spoils." Undulating against his human, Gerard added, "And you're alive, and your enemy is not. You're the victor."

Britt's eyes darkened as the smell of arousal perfumed the air. "Hell, yeah." With a hungry smile curving his lips, he asked, "How fast can we get to your bathroom? I want to clean you and inspect every inch of you."

Taking that as a personal challenge, Gerard showed Britt

the quickest back route home that he knew.

To Gerard's pleasure, Britt rewarded him and then some.

ABOUT THE AUTHOR

Charlie started writing fantasy when she was eight, and after stumbling onto her first erotic romance at age nineteen, she realized her true calling. She now focuses on writing gay erotic romance, normally of the paranormal variety, with heroes of all kinds. With the help and support of her husband, Charlie finally fulfilled one of her life-long goals . . . move to acreage with her horses. You can often find her curled up with her laptop and a cup of tea or glass of wine, creating her next adventure. Charlie enjoys exploring the mountains of her new Oregon home on horseback, 4-wheeler, or motorcycle.

She can be reached at ch.richards2010@yahoo.com

Or visit her at www.charlie-richards.com.

www.ingramcontent.com/pod-product-compliance
Lightning Source LLC
Chambersburg PA
CBHW070540130626
46555CB00003B/1505